THE DIZ AND DEE HOLIDAY MYSTERIES

ANNIE REED

T**V***Ink*
Thunder Valley

PRAISE FOR ANNIE REED

"One of the best writers I've come across in years. Annie excels at whatever genre of fiction she chooses to write."

— KRISTINE KATHRYN RUSCH, AWARD-WINNING WRITER/EDITOR

"You can't go wrong with Annie Reed. Her deftly-crafted tales—with characters as memorable as the stories themselves—far surpass most of what's out there. She deserves a wide audience."

— MICHAEL J. TOTTEN, AUTHOR

"Annie's writing is magic, seriously."

— ROBERT J. MCCARTER, AUTHOR

"Annie Reed is considered by many to be one of the best new writers appearing in fiction."

— DEAN WESLEY SMITH, EDITOR
PULPHOUSE FICTION MAGAZINE

The Diz and Dee Holiday Mysteries
Copyright © 2024 Annie Reed

Published by Thunder Valley Ink
Cover art Copyright ©Cresta Willis/bigstockphotos.com,
BasheeraDesigns/bigstockphotos.com
Cover and layout Copyright © 2024 Thunder Valley Ink

For more information on the author, go to www.annie-reed.com.

ISBN: 978-1-954460-03-4

CONTENTS

INTRODUCTION

Diz and Dee started out as a crayon doodle on a butcher paper tablecloth.

I was out with my family enjoying a nice Italian dinner (eggplant parmesan for me) in one of those restaurants where the tablecloths are white butcher paper and the restaurant provides a few crayons to keep the kiddies entertained until the food arrives. I'm easily distracted, and I like to doodle as much as your average six-year-old budding artist.

What I ended up doodling was a curly haired, mullet-wearing elf with pointy ears, freckles, a five o'clock shadow, and a grin.

That little bit of butcher paper came home along with a take-out box of leftover eggplant parmesan. I ate the food, put the doodle in a desk drawer, and promptly forgot about the whole thing.

Or so I thought.

Over the next year or so, in between other projects, I

played around with a practice novel as I got to know my mullet-wearing elf. Along the way he lost the grin, the freckles, and the curly hair, not to mention the five o'clock shadow. He also gained a partner—human precog Dee, who became the voice of the Diz and Dee mysteries.

But it wasn't until I wrote "The Case of the Missing Elf" that the whole thing fell into place.

This volume contains all Diz and Dee's holiday adventures. Christmas, Valentine's Day, St. Patrick's Day, Easter, and New Year's Eve. There's even a brand-new Thanksgiving mystery that's only available in this collection.

Diz and Dee have moved beyond solving mysteries solely on the holidays. They've gone to an anime convention looking for a very special missing ceramic statue, and they've gone on the hunt for a missing method actor trying to get into character as a werewolf. But I always have the most fun writing about my intrepid detectives when their mysteries intersect with the holidays. I hope you enjoy the stories in this collection as much as I did when I was writing them. Happy holidays!

—Annie Reed
Reno, Nevada
November 24, 2019

THE CASE OF THE
MISSING ELF

I was having a non-argument argument with my partner about whether we should get a Christmas tree for the office when the front door opened and a whole passel of elves piled in.

Up front, I should tell you that my partner is an elf. A tall one. Broad-shouldered, pointy-eared, strong-jawed, and with the most drop-dead gorgeous blue eyes I've ever seen. You might be thinking Legolas from those movies, but Diz is more The Rock than Orlando Bloom. He even has The Rock's glower. The cinnamon and marshmallow-colored mullet, though—that's all Diz's own.

Yeah, I know. A mullet. But considering how great the rest of him looks, who am I to complain?

Together, Diz and I run a private detective agency called D & D Investigations out of a former bakery in a rundown neighborhood on the mainland side of More-town Bay. I'm Dee, the other D in D & D. I'm not an elf.

Or a dwarf. Or a fairy or any one of a hundred other kinds of magic folk who call the area around the Bay home. I'm a plain old vanilla human with curly brown hair that tends to frizz when it's humid, which is just about all the time. I also have a touch of precognition I've yet to learn how to control any better than my hair.

"You find missing people?" the nearest elf in the pack said.

I looked down at him. Unlike Diz, who's a good foot taller than my medium height, these elves were all way shorter than I am. I counted seven of the mini elves. They all wore variations of the same outfit: forest-green pants, red-and-green shirts that were more tunic than shirt, and red, green, or white scarves. The elf who asked me whether we find missing people had curly salt-and-pepper hair peeking out from beneath a red knit hat with a white pom-pom on top. They made the office look like a seasonal munchkin convention.

"Uh, yeah," I said. I resisted the urge to point to the lettering beneath the agency name on the plate glass window of our office—Missing Persons Are Our Specialty. We'd paid extra for that, but no one ever seemed to read it.

The elf behind the guy with the red knit hat elbowed him. "I don't care what you say, this can't be the right place," he said in a stage whisper I could hear fine even though his voice sounded like he'd just taken a hit of helium. "Just look at it."

The rest of the elves nodded and muttered among

themselves. Except for the elf with the red hat, they all sounded like helium addicts.

I glanced over at Diz, expecting to see his everyday glower amped up to a killer scowl. My partner and patience aren't even on a handshake basis. Diz was born without that sense of serenity that's second nature to most wood elves. Stuff gets to him. He left his clan's home on Marlette Island years before I was even born. Life among the trees probably drove him batty. Lord knows why he puts up with me, not that I'd complain about that either. I know when I've got a good thing going.

One of the things Diz can't stand is a client who won't get to the point. Between the scowl and the lack of patience and the elfen strength, Diz can be flat out intimidating. That's what made him such a kickass interrogator when we were both with the cops. Now that we're detecting on our own and can't afford to scare potential clients away, I do most of the initial interviews. I can be kind of a smartass, but at least I'm nice about it.

Most of the time.

But now, instead of having to deflect Diz from going into full scowl mode, I caught him in a near-grin.

"You're smiling," I said to him.

The grin disappeared. "Am not."

I lifted an eyebrow. I'm not sure why my partner doesn't like to admit when he's having a good time, but far be it for me to let him get away with it.

"Right," I said. "And I'm Santa."

Immediately, all the pint-sized elves in the office went quiet.

"What?" I said to the elves who were all giving me the evil eye.

"You are not Santa," the elf with the red knit hat said.

"No!" chorused the rest of the little elves.

"You don't even have any Christmas decorations!" said the little elf behind Red Hat.

The elves all nodded in agreement.

"I have this." I pointed toward the sad-looking little miniature pine tree in a candy-cane striped pot I'd picked up at the Asian store next to the office. The tree had little red ornaments wired to its spindly branches and a red bow stuck on one side of the pot. Even I had to admit it was lame as holiday decorations went.

That's why I wanted to put up a Christmas tree. Diz had pointed out that my sad little potted pine was a prime example of why I shouldn't be allowed around plants. I'd pointed out to him that Christmas trees were already pretty much dead, so anything I did to it couldn't possibly be worse. That's when his latent wood elf rose to the surface. Diz told me he refused to have a sacrificial tree ensconced—ensconced, mind you—in his office.

Did I tell you that back when we were both cops, I was the only one who could put up with him for more than a week at a time?

Of course, he was the only one who could put up with me for more than a week at a time, too. Maybe that's why we're still working together, although I'd like to think there's a little more to it than that.

"That," Red Hat said, pointing an accusatory finger at my poor potted pine, "is not evidence of the true Christmas spirit."

"What's the Christmas spirit got to do with why you're all here, anyway?" I asked.

"How can you find Santa if you don't have the Christmas spirit?"

I blinked. "Come again? You want us to find Santa? The Santa?"

"He's missing," said the little elf behind Red Hat.

"And we're running out of time," said another one somewhere in the chorus. "It's almost Christmas Eve."

"Huh," I said.

I took a better look at the half-size elves. All dressed in red and green. Check. All had rosy cheeks. Check. All their clothes looked a size too big because... they've been working too hard getting ready for the big day to hit the milk and cookies?

"That would make you Santa's elves," I said.

"Yes," said Red Hat with a proud little grin.

Okay. I reminded myself that I'd seen stranger things. Not many, true, but I live in kind of a strange time when magic folk don't bother to hide themselves much anymore. It makes life interesting.

I managed to keep from asking where they stashed the reindeer, but it was a close call. "I think we'd better sit down," I said.

Red Hat and the rest of Santa's elves eyed the two straight-back chairs and the secondhand loveseat we kept in the office for clients. Not exactly pint-sized elf accommodations.

"Okay," I said. "Then I need to sit down."

The front office had an old wooden desk and a semi-battered executive chair. I plopped down in the chair. Diz leaned against the door frame to our back office.

I could have ushered the elves into the back office, but I prefer the front office for client meetings. The back office only has a couple of used secretarial desks, a file cabinet we rarely use, and our computer equipment. It's not the tidiest of rooms. As former cops, Diz and I are allergic to paperwork. Plus, the ghostly scent of Baked Goods Past tends to be a bit too tempting, at least for me. Diz never gains weight no matter what he eats. He tells me it's an elf thing. I wish it was a Dee thing too.

"What we're about to tell you has to remain strictly confidential," Red Hat said.

"No problem," I said, settling back in my chair. "Why don't you start out by telling us your names."

Red Hat turned out to be Snickerdoodle. I think I liked Red Hat better.

The rest of the elves were Sugarcane (the little elf who'd elbowed Red Hat—er, Snickerdoodle), Merry (who was a boyish-looking girl; only her rosier-than-everyone-else's lips gave her away), Gumdrop, Doodles (no relation to Snickerdoodle, he said), Noggin, and Hal.

"Hal?" I asked.

The elf scrunched up his rosy little button nose. "My parents were unconventional."

"Tell me about it," Diz muttered.

I'm one of a handful of people who know that Diz was named after Dizzy Gillespie, the jazz great. Diz had chubby cheeks when he was born, and his jazz-loving parents took it as a sign. Diz's full name is Dizzy G. He's grown out of the chubby-cheek phase. Now he's got cheekbones to die for, but he's stuck with the name.

"So, Snickerdoodle," I said. "You want us to find Santa? We don't normally work at the North Pole." I wasn't sure I even had the right clothes for it. Diz might be able to tolerate all sorts of weather, no problem, but I was born and bred in the Pacific Northwest, and I've lived in Moretown Bay all my life. I'm a rainy-season girl. I don't do snow.

"Well..." A look passed between Snickerdoodle and the rest of the elves. I knew that look. It meant the other shoe was about to drop. "You won't be looking for Santa per se."

Per se. Oh, how I love that phrase. It means "I'm lying to you, but not really."

"Maybe you'd better start from the top," I said.

"Santa's on sabbatical this year."

Sabbatical? "He can do that?"

"Sure," said Sugarcane. "Everybody needs a vacation."

"He only works one night a year," Diz said.

Snickerdoodle snorted. "That's what everyone thinks. Santa's the CEO of a global operation, but nobody ever considers that. He works 24/7 twelve months a year to make sure every good little boy and girl around the world gets what they want for Christmas."

"But not everyone in the world believes in Christmas or Santa," I said.

Snickerdoodle nodded. "Our foreign office handles that. We have agreements with all sorts of holiday providers. Hal's second in command of our legal division up at the North Pole."

Huh. "You're a lawyer?" I asked Hal.

"Can't make toys worth a darn," Hal said. "My parents sent me to law school."

"That's good to know." I wondered if I needed to double check our standard retainer agreement before I asked Snickerdoodle to sign it. "So with Santa on sabbatical, who's actually going to... uh, drive the reindeer this year?"

"That would be Norman," Merry said with a sigh.

"Norman?"

"Santa's stand in," Snickerdoodle said. "Santa's a little taller than the rest of us. Norman's the only one who can fill Santa's suit."

"And, let me guess. Norman's who you want us to find."

Snickerdoodle nodded. "Delivering toys on Christmas Eve is a big job, so we gave him a couple of extra weeks off after Thanksgiving to burn off a little steam. Whenever he went on vacation before, he ate his way through the Southeast."

"He likes those food challenge shows on TV," said Gumdrop. "Norman thinks he could be a championship eater if he just put his mind to it."

"Besides, he needs to put on a little weight to be Santa's stand in," Merry said. "Santa is kind of... jolly."

Rolly poly, more like it. "Only Norman didn't come back," I said. "Why do you think he's somewhere in this area?" It was pretty easy to see where the story was going, and hey, I'm not a detective for nothing.

Merry and Gumdrop shared a look, but it was Doodles who spoke up. "He sent me a text," the elf said. "He lost two food challenges in a row. Got pretty down on himself. Said he was going to try drinking his way through the northwest instead."

Oh, boy.

If Norman really was here, he had to be at the Holly Jolly Eggnog Festival.

Back in July, the Moretown Bay Chamber of Commerce decided that nothing said Christmas like a spiked eggnog competition. As if the shopping district down by the wharf wasn't already packed to the gills during the holiday season, this year the streets would be jammed with drunken eggnog connoisseurs going head to head with determined last-minute bargain hunters.

The festival had started the day before and ran until four in the afternoon on Christmas Eve, when the grand prize would be awarded and the competitors would close up shop and go home to nurse their holiday hangovers. While the festival didn't have an official drinking competition, it definitely had an abundance of alcoholic eggnog. It made sense that eggnog with a little something extra would be the drink of choice for a wayward Christmas elf.

"Have you tried looking for him?" I asked.

"Are you kidding?" Noggin asked. He was the smallest of all the elves. "We'd get crushed by all those people." He shuddered.

"We all live up at the North Pole for a reason," Merry said.

Gumdrop nodded. "Nobody steps on us."

"And we have a great benefits package," said Hal.

"Really?" The only real benefit I had with the detective agency, outside of being my own boss (which was pretty cool, even though I was broke half the time) was leaning against the door jam, trying to look glowery. I cleared my throat and tried to stop dreaming of affordable healthcare and a retirement plan. "So, we'll need a description of Norman, and a picture if you have one."

They didn't, but Doodles drew a pretty good sketch of Norman on a piece of printer paper. Hal spent a few minutes studying our retainer agreement before he told Snickerdoodle he had no problems with it.

After the elves gave me a contact number and one day's fees in cash (which I scrutinized to make sure wasn't play money), they filed out the door.

I turned to Diz. "What do you say, partner? Should we go find ourselves a missing elf?"

As a general rule, I try to avoid holiday crowds. I've been single all my life. Oh, sure, I've had boyfriends now and then, but the longest relationship I've had is with my cat, and she ignores me half the time. I'm good with that. My idea of an exciting evening is to curl up with a good book and a monster-sized diet soda. Of course, I wouldn't mind having a certain elf share more than office space with me. Who wouldn't? I mean, look at those ears. Until I started working with Diz, I never thought a pointy ear could be so alluring. You have no idea how often I've had to stuff my hands in my pockets just to keep myself from embarrassing us both.

Where was I again?

Oh, yeah. Holiday crowds.

I don't do crowds well. I used to be a cop. I used to carry a gun. Sometimes I still do. For the sake of every holiday shopper and eggnog imbiber at the Holly Jolly Eggnog Festival, it was probably a good thing I'd left my gun in the safe back at the office.

"No amount of money is worth this," I said after I'd been elbowed for the umpteenth time trying to make my way to yet another eggnog vendor to show Doodles' sketch of Norman to yet another harried barkeep.

"It's not just the money," Diz said. "If we don't find Norman and dry him out, there won't be a Christmas this year."

I hadn't thought of that. "Don't you think they have a backup elf?"

"Would they be here if they did?"

True. "Doesn't seem like a wise business plan." You'd think they could just call Santa off sabbatical if it was an emergency.

"Look out!" Diz pulled me back against him just in

time to keep me from being brained by a guy carrying a new set of skis and poles on his shoulder.

"Thanks," I said, trying to ignore just how good Diz felt up against my back even through my jacket. I settled for glaring at the guy with the skis. I could understand why the North Pole elves thought they'd get trampled down here. "How are we going to find one elf in all this?"

"You're not getting anything?"

That was Diz's way of asking me if I had any sort of a precog sense about our missing Santa stand-in. I'd tried back at the office after I'd looked at the sketch, but all I got for my trouble was the beginning of a headache. "Nope," I said. "You see anything?"

Like all elves, Diz had amazing eyesight, plus he was taller than most of the people jamming the street. The festival took up the entire two blocks of the wharf-side shopping district, and the city had wisely blocked off the street from traffic. Booths and shops selling everything from original artwork to handmade clothes and jewelry to fresh fish to designer coffee on both sides of the street were doing bang up business. Most of the eggnog vendors had set up their own booths or wagons in the middle of the cobblestone street, but a few were doing business out of the local pubs. The crowd was so thick Norman could have walked past me and I would never even see him. Diz had a better shot, or so I hoped.

"Nope." Diz nodded at an apartment building at the end of the block. "I might do better up there."

The apartment building was a five-story brick relic rehabbed into a bohemian artists' paradise. The residents had decorated the outside of their windows with an eclectic mix of traditional and New Age designs, everything from a crescent moon in a Santa hat smiling at a Betty Boop-ish cartoon cutout in a holiday outfit that would have made a Playboy bunny blush, to one-half of a completely decorated artificial Christmas tree wired to a window frame.

"Don't tell me you're—" I said.

"Up there," Diz said again.

"You're going to take the elevator, right?"

"It's quicker my way."

Quicker, yes. Easier? Not if you were me standing on the sidewalk watching my partner scale the outside of a five-story building like he was Spiderman.

Diz tells me it's an elf thing. Something that all wood elves can do. Probably comes from decades of practice scaling trees, but trees have branches. Buildings don't. Buildings have teeny, tiny finger and toe holds, and the ground below isn't dirt and trees leaves but cement.

Diz has yet to fall, at least that he's told me. Personally, I think he just likes showing off, especially because he knows I get nervous watching him. Does that mean he likes me in more than a business partner kind of way? If we were in grade school, would he be pulling my pigtails?

Before I finished telling him to be careful, Diz was off through the crowd, then up the side of the building. I don't think I breathed until he reached the top. Damn elf was going to be the death of me one day.

I didn't need elf vision to see the grin on his face. Diz

didn't smile often, but boy, when he did, he did a great job of it. Now he was looking right at me and smiling.

Huh. Something told me he'd just pulled my pigtail.

I started to smile back when the air in front of me wavered, almost like little heat waves coming off the cold cement sidewalk beneath my feet.

Oh, no. Not now.

Before I could find a nice, safe spot in the crowd, the vision took me.

Sometimes my precog sense gives me just a little hint, like a whiff of something that smells good but not enough of a scent to identify what that something is. At other times it's like a flashbulb's gone off in my brain and I get quick little disjointed images of things. I can usually handle myself when my precog sense only gives me light stuff like that. When I get in trouble is when a minimovie version of my precog sense slams itself over reality.

That's what happened to me in the middle of the Holly Jolly Eggnog Festival. One minute I was holding my own—pretty much anyway—against a throng of holiday shoppers and eggnog drinkers, and the next I was in a crowded restaurant with a massive plate of chili-cheese fries and hotdogs in front of my face.

The first few bites of chili went down okay. Better than okay. I felt invigorated. I picked up a handful of fries and shoved them in my mouth, and the people at the next table turned around to watch. Two hotdogs were next, and a few more people wandered over to see what I was doing. I ate more chili, and when I looked up, the crowd watching me had grown. By the time the plate was half empty, the crowd was chanting, "You can do it!" I'd never felt so good and so full at the same time.

Somewhere in the background, I heard violins playing, then a chorale joined in as the strains of a familiar Christmas carol overtook the chanting of the crowd. I looked up and saw a high domed ceiling covered in antique gold with a faint burgundy pattern. Long curtains hung over the walls at the sides of the dome, and I could smell expensive perfume and pine trees. Real Christmas trees.

Then the vision jerked me back to the restaurant. The plate was empty, and people were clapping me on the back. A light bulb went off in my face as someone took my picture.

The light bulb flash snapped me back to reality.

I was against the side of a building, out of the crowd, and Diz was holding me. My left hand hurt, and so did the back of my head. People gave us a wide berth, either because they thought I'd had a fit and it might be catching, or because Diz was in full glare mode.

"I'm okay." I shook my hand. Did somebody step on me while I was out? That might explain Diz's glare. "I might never eat another hotdog again," I said, "but I'm okay."

"Vision?"

I nodded. "Yeah, and it was a doozy." I looked up into concerned blue eyes and grinned. "But I think I know where our errant elf is going to be."

THE MORETOWN BAY symphony orchestra gave afternoon performances every day during the entire week before Christmas. Diz and I were outside the concert hall when that afternoon's performance let out. It didn't take long for Diz to spot Norman in the crowd.

The wayward elf did look an awful lot like like a department store Santa, only his white beard was real, as was his jolly round belly—made rounder, no doubt, by an over-abundance of hotdogs and chili-cheese fries— and he was about a foot shorter than your average Santa impersonator. He wasn't dressed in Christmas red and green, though. Instead, he had on a blue plaid flannel shirt, blue jeans, and a denim jacket. If it wasn't for the rosy red cheeks and button nose, he could have been any smaller-than-normal lumberjack out for a little holiday culture.

He gave Diz and I a wary look when we approached him on the street. I held up the sketch Doodles had drawn. "A few of your friends are a little concerned about you," I said. "They asked us to find you."

For a minute, I thought he might run. He must have thought better about it because he just looked deflated, like a kid caught being truant. "Well, you found me," he said. His voice didn't sound helium enhanced like the other elves. No wonder he could lose himself in a crowd. "Now what?"

"They'd like you to go back home with them." I

glanced around and saw a few curious onlookers. "So you can go back to work," I said, trying to keep the conversation as generic as possible.

Norman looked at me. There was nothing jolly in his expression. "What if I don't want to?"

I thought about all the kids who wouldn't have a merry Christmas if Norman didn't step into Santa's red suit and take his place in the sleigh behind eight tiny reindeer. "You want to talk about it?" I asked.

Norman shrugged. "Sure. Just so long as you don't try to kidnap me."

"No kidnapping," I said. "Why would you think we'd do a thing like that?"

Norman glanced at my partner. Diz was standing next to us, scowling at anyone who got too close. I raised an eyebrow at him. "You're scaring the elf," I said.

Diz got the hint. "No kidnapping," he said.

The three of us—Diz, Norman, and I—ended up in a coffee shop a block away from the concert hall. "A Christmas symphony isn't exactly the kind of place I'd expect to see an elf who told his friends he was off to an eggnog festival," I said.

Norman made a face at his coffee cup. "I thought that would keep them from looking for me," he said. "They don't like crowds of people."

"I can understand that," I said. "But why give them a clue that would lead them right here? Why not send them on a wild goose chase to South Carolina?"

"He wanted to be found," Diz said.

Diz was right. I could see it in Norman's expression. "You got me there," Norman said.

Talk about a conflicted elf.

"They're counting on you," I said. "It's just for this year."

"Is that what they told you?" Norman shook his head. "Leave it to Snickerdoodle not to tell the whole tale. That is who you talked to, right?"

I nodded. "Who is he?"

"Santa's chief of staff." Norman took a sip of coffee. "Should have ordered hot chocolate," he muttered.

He didn't sound like an elf who'd go on a bender. "Tell me, did you actually compete in any eggnog drinking contests?"

Norman actually shivered. "Heavens, no. I can't stand the stuff. My mother used to make it with raw eggs. Dreadful."

"But you ate your weight in hotdogs and chili-cheese fries."

Norman's bushy white eyebrows rose on his forehead. "How did you know that?"

"There's more to Dee than meets the eye," Diz said.

From Diz that was almost a testimonial. Had the holiday spirit actually gotten to my grumpy partner? First, a smile from five stories up. Now an actual compliment.

"Look," Norman said. "Every ten years, I fill in for the big man behind the sleigh. I eat his cookies, drink his milk, leave presents signed with his name, and on Christmas morning, who does everyone thank? Him, not me. No child has ever heard of an elf named Norman, but in a hole-in-the-wall restaurant in Charlotte, South Carolina, my name and picture is on a Wall of Fame with only eight other people. I'm one of only nine who beat that food challenge. Me. Norman. Not Santa."

He shut his mouth with an almost audible snap, and stared down at his coffee like he'd said too much. I thought he'd said what he should have said years ago.

"And after that happened, after people applauded you," I said, "you couldn't stand the idea of putting on that red suit and pretending to be Santa for a night."

Norman pointed a finger at me. "You got it."

"You're going to disappoint a lot of kids if you don't."

For someone whose nose and cheeks made them look perpetually jolly, Norman was doing one fine job of impersonating a depressed person.

"What if I can work something out?" I asked. "I'm pretty good at negotiating." That had been my strong suit back when Diz and I had been cops. He'd intimidate the bad guys, then I'd come in and get them to talk in exchange for a little leniency when it came time to sentencing.

"What do you have in mind?" Norman asked.

I leaned in close and explained my plan.

NORMAN SAT in front of my office desk in one of the client chairs. His feet almost touched the floor. The other elves gathered around the other client chair where Snickerdoodle sat. I'd put a step stool in front of the chair so that the shorter elf could climb into the chair.

"Here's what I propose," I said. "Norman here would like a life of his own. Right now he'd like that life to include participating in eating challenges during the off season at the North Pole."

"His employment contract provides for two weeks of paid vacation per year, with an additional two weeks on the years Santa takes a sabbatical," Hal said.

"That's more than fair," Snickerdoodle said. "The rest of us only get two weeks off. The North Pole is a very busy place year round."

"True," I said. "But the rest of you don't have to become someone else every ten years." I paused. "One very beloved someone else. Norman works very hard that one night and gets none of the credit. Food competition, as it turns out, is something that he's very good at in his own right. I bet none of you could eat a dozen hot dogs and five pounds of chili-cheese fries in one sitting."

Merry actually looked a little green around the gills. I didn't blame her.

"In exchange," I went on, "Norman will accompany you back to the North Pole and be Santa this year, and he agrees to never pull another disappearing act on you for as long as he's required to be Santa's stand in."

None of the elves looked too happy, including Norman, but I'd explained to him the art of compromise.

"You don't have anyone else to do the job, do you?" I asked.

"No," Snickerdoodle said.

"Not even Santa?" I asked.

Noggin shuddered. "No one disturbs Santa during his sabbatical. Not even Mrs. Claus."

Okay, I so didn't want to think too closely about that. "Do you think we have a deal here?"

A significant glance passed between Snickerdoodle and Hal. "I could revise his employment contract," Hal finally said. "But we'd have to include a confidentiality clause. The rest of the elves get wind of this, they'll all want a more lenient vacation policy. They might even want to—"

"Take sabbaticals?" I asked.

Snickerdoodle shot me a glare that rivaled one of Diz's better ones. If Norman hadn't been grinning at me, I would have been worried my stocking would be stuffed with coal come Christmas morning.

"It's a deal," Snickerdoodle said.

"Great!" I said.

Gumdrop pulled a whistle out of his pocket. I didn't hear a thing when he blew it, but a few seconds later, I swore I heard sounds coming from the roof.

"Time to go," Snickerdoodle said to Norman. "At least you've got your padding set."

Norman shook my hand, and the elves all piled out of the front door and headed toward the side of the building. A moment later, I heard more sounds from the roof, then a muffled, "Ho, Ho, Ho!"

I looked at Diz, my eyes wide. "You don't suppose there were eight tiny reindeer and a sleigh up there, do you?"

He gave me one of his very rare lopsided grins. "You never know."

～

I GOT BACK to the agency on Christmas Eve after delivering a Christmas card to the woman who runs the Asian store next door to find a fully decorated tree in the corner of the front office.

"What's this?" I asked Diz.

He was sitting in my semi-battered executive chair with his boot-clad feet propped up on my desk. "A compromise."

What?

He gestured at the base of the tree. Instead of a stand, I saw a wooden tub filled with dirt.

Diz had bought me a live pine tree.

"You know I'm not good with green things," I said.

"I'll take care of it, and after New Year's, we can take it outside and plant it."

I didn't know what to say. "What made you change your mind?"

He got up with one of those fluid moves that make me feel like the most clumsy creature on the planet. He walked to my side of the desk and put his arm around my shoulders. "You did good," he said. "A lot of kids are going to have a Merry Christmas thanks to you." He dropped a light kiss on the top of my head. "I thought you deserved what you wanted for Christmas, too."

I stood there with my mouth hanging open and a

foolish grin on my face. A Christmas tree and a kiss from my grumpy partner. Okay, he kissed me on the top of my head, but it was a still a kiss.

This might turn out to be a pretty darn good Christmas after all.

OMENS AND ORACLES
AND EROS, OH MY

I t's not every day a Greek god walks through a girl's front door.

My partner and I run a detective agency out of an old storefront half a mile from the ferry landing on the mainland side of Moretown Bay. The neighborhood is rundown urban with a touch of whimsical eclectic. The shop next door sells everything Asian, from manga to anime to imported CD soundtracks side by side with things like shrimp chips and lychee jellies. The masseuse across the street has her front door decorated with purple glitter and glow-in-the-dark stars. Every time one of her customers opens that door, enough aromatherapy candle smoke escapes to engulf the neighborhood in a cloud of calm. Or passion. I'm pretty sure on those days she provides more than a simple massage. I don't intend to find out. She seems like a nice enough woman, but I'm not that starved for affection. Not yet.

I didn't recognize the guy who walked in my office

like he owned the place, not right away, anyway. Who'd have thought you'd find a god wandering around a neighborhood like this? The sidewalk in front of our office looks like concrete accordion pleats, and I'm pretty sure a family of four is living in the panel van permanently parked at the back of the municipal lot at the end of the block.

Plus, the guy wasn't dressed in a diaper and carting a bow and arrows. Even a detective needs at least a couple clues.

"You find lost people?" he asked, his tone more than a little upper crust.

"We do." I resisted the urge to look at the plate glass window at the front of the office. The name on that window was D & D Investigations and underneath: Missing Persons Are Our Specialty.

I'm Dee, one half of D & D. Diz, short for Dizzy G, is the other half. Diz is an elf. I'm not. I get along with most people. He glowers. He's also built like The Rock, and that makes him more than a little intimidating. Which is why I'm the one who meets with potential clients. If I let Diz do the meet and greet, we'd both be begging the police department for our old jobs back.

"I need you to find someone," the guy said.

I smiled my most competent, professional detective smile. "Have a seat."

The guy sat, rather gingerly, in one of the two client chairs in front of my desk. The chairs were straight back, fake leather armchairs, comfortable but definitely not high rent. Nothing in our office was high rent. I had no doubt the guy's tailored suit cost more than the monthly rent on my office-slash-apartment, and I could have eaten for a couple of weeks at the best restaurants More-town Bay has to offer on what he must have spent on his shoes.

"Who's missing?" I asked him.

"My youngest daughter," he said. "Dyte." He pronounced it DIE-tee. "She's named after her grandmother."

Dyte. Unusual name. Really unusual name.

Wait a minute.

I'm not a detective for nothing. The guy in my client chair had the kind of ethereal beauty that marked him as something other than a mere mortal like me. He had an angelic face, and tight little ringlet curls hugged his head. Strip away the fancy suit, slap the guy in a diaper, hand him a bow and some heart-tipped arrows, and oh yeah—he was the absolute personification of every cheesy Valentine's Day card I'd ever gotten as a kid.

So when he said his daughter was named after her grandmother, did that mean Dyte as in Aphrodite?

Holy shit. I had an actual Greek god sitting in my client chair. I wondered where he stowed his wings.

"You're Cupid?" I managed to choke out.

He sniffed. "Eros. I prefer Eros. Cupid is so"—he made a vague gesture with one hand—"common."

Our office used to house a bakery. The space had been gutted and fresh paint slapped on the walls before we moved in, but there were days when the air in the Bay was hot enough and humid enough that I could smell glazed donuts. Now I smelled chocolate. Specifically, the kind of overwhelming chocolate overkill you got when you lifted the lid off a box of Valentine's candy. Maybe Cupid—er, Eros—brought it with him, his own personal aromatherapy.

"My daughter hasn't been seen or heard from in a week. Can you find her or not?" Eros asked.

Okay. I might have been a tad overwhelmed at meeting one of the Greek gods in the flesh, so to speak, but that didn't mean I was a pushover. I didn't automatically say yes to anyone. "Give me some details," I said.

He settled back a little in the chair. "She is a very headstrong girl. She has been since she was old enough to say no to her mother and I. She also has the best head for business of anyone in the family, and believe me when I tell you it's a very large family."

Believe him, I did. Eros wasn't the God of Love for nothing. Even though the police department didn't have many dealings with the old gods—most of them lived in Europe these days—back when Diz and I were still on the force, rumors had circulated from one law enforcement agency to the next about the exploits of old Eros here. If only ten percent of the gossip about the guy sitting in my office had any basis in reality, he had fathered enough children throughout the millennia to populate a third-world country.

"How old is she?" I asked.

"Seventeen."

"And her mother?"

He gave me a withering look. "You must know the story."

I dimly remembered the story of Eros and Psyche. Like a good many stories about the old gods, the tale involved jealousy, love, obsession, betrayal, revenge, impossible tasks, a good deal of death, both of the little d and capital D kind, reconciliation, and oh yes, a happy ending. Sounds like the plot line of any daytime soap, only without the happy ending part. Not that I've watched a lot of soap operas. Really.

Short version was that Eros fell in love with Psyche, a mortal, who eventually became a god and married Eros, all with the blessing of no less than Zeus himself who'd been known to dabble in the mortal realm. I guessed the randy among the old gods had to stick up for each other.

That made Dyte a god in her own right. Fun.

"Do you believe foul play was involved?" I asked him.

"No." He sighed, and his angelically rounded face drooped a little. "She issued an ultimatum to her mother and I, and when we refused, she stomped off in a huff. She hasn't been in touch with us since."

So Dyte had a temper. More fun.

"It might help to know what the ultimatum was all about," I said.

He seemed to squirm without actually moving. Apparently gods could do that.

"This infernal holiday," he finally said.

I had an LOL Cats day-by-day calendar on my desk, a Christmas present from my cat courtesy of Diz. He told me knowing what cats want to give their people on major holidays is an elf thing. I'm not sure I believe him, but hey—it got my business partner to pay a little bit of attention to me in a non-business kind of way, so who am I to call him on that little bit of subterfuge.

Have I mentioned that Diz is one-hundred percent gorgeous? My partner could give old Eros a run for his money. Diz just never seems interested in anyone, least of all me. Hope, though, springs eternal.

According to my calendar, today was January 29th. I didn't think the holiday Eros was talking about was Ground Hog Day.

"Your daughter doesn't have a boyfriend for Valentine's Day and is what... worried she'll have to spend the day dateless?"

Eros looked down his cute little aristocratic nose at me. "Hardly."

The shoulders of his charcoal grey suit jacket shifted and something rustled against the material.

Wow. He really did have wings under all that tailored wool. I must have annoyed him enough that he ruffled his feathers without thinking about it.

"Exactly the opposite," he said. "Dyte believes that The Holiday is a crass commercialization of our family's —of my—image, and she wants it to stop."

I didn't blame her. I didn't much like Valentine's Day either, and the iconic image of my father wasn't plastered all over the place to help greeting card companies, florists, and jewelers haul in the big bucks on that very special commercialized day of love.

"What does she want you to do about it?" I asked.

"Cancel a few thousand licensing agreements, which would not only expose our family to breach-of-contract lawsuits around the globe but severely impact our earnings, not to mention potential earnings, for the foreseeable future."

Come again? "You have licensing agreements?"

His suit jacket shrugged by itself again. More feather ruffling. "If someone wants to use my image to sell a product, why shouldn't I profit from it? Tithes and offerings are not what they once were."

No kidding. I guess the old gods didn't have a lot of worshippers these days.

"I thought you said she had a good head for business. What she wants doesn't sound like good business."

"She seems to think I should be able to make the agreements simply disappear with the individuals on the other end being none the wiser."

"You can't?"

"There are consequences for the misuse of power, even for the gods."

"In other words, you have to play by the rules, and she doesn't understand that."

"Do children ever?"

I didn't know, at least not from personal experience. The closest I had to a kid was my cat, and as long as I kept her in tuna and catnip, all was right in her world.

"There's something I don't understand," I said. "You're a god. You can do all sorts of god stuff. But you want me to find her? Me?"

He glared at me. Diz could do a better glare, but he

31

doesn't go around shooting people with arrows. Not that I know about, anyway. If I didn't want to find one of Eros' arrows in the middle of my back and myself with a sudden crush on the masseuse across the street, I'd better behave.

"I am under certain constraints," he said. "I do love my daughter. Yes, she's headstrong and determined, but she gets that from her mother."

Just from her mother. Sure.

"The world today is not what it once was," he said, his voice wistful now. "People, by and large, do not respect the old gods and certainly not our offspring. She doesn't understand that. I don't want her hurt."

I sighed. I knew he'd just made a play for my sympathy, but that didn't change the fact that arrogant or not, god or not, at his core, Eros was a father whose daughter was missing. He was asking for my help. But he still hadn't explained why he was looking for help in the human realm. He was a god. If he couldn't go look for her because of whatever "constraints" were preventing him, couldn't he—I don't know—maybe get another god to do the job? There had to be a god for runaway children. Back when I'd read about these guys in school, it seemed like there was a god for everything. Except maybe stubbed toes.

"I don't understand why you think I can help." I spread my hands out, palms up. "I'm mortal. You're a god. She's a god. I'm pretty sure you have more resources than I do."

"The Oracle," he said, as if that explained it all.

I arched an eyebrow.

"I was told to enlist the aid of a mortal woman without using my usual 'powers of persuasion,'" he said.

Alrighty, then. No arrows in the back. Check. I was good with that.

"You were the first detective listed in the D's," he said.

"The D's?"

"Dyte's name begins with a D. It was a good omen."

Oh, goody. Omens and Oracles and a petulant runaway teenage god. My day was really looking up.

I might need a massage after all.

"YOU TOOK THE CASE?" Diz glowered at me. The effect was spoiled by my cat, who'd deigned to saunter downstairs from my second floor apartment and was currently perched on Diz's shoulder, rubbing her head against the side of his face.

My cat had all the luck.

"I didn't think it was smart to say no to a god," I said.

Diz didn't look convinced.

"He paid us an advance." No change to the intensity of my partner's glare. "In cash."

D & D Investigations was not the most successful detective agency in Moretown Bay. Most months we barely scraped by, and so far, the first month of the new year had seen our cash flow drop to next to nothing. We couldn't afford to turn down a paying customer.

Diz knew that. He just didn't like it.

We decided to start our search for Dyte the way we started every case. I powered up my on-the-edge-of-obsolescence laptop and opened an internet browser.

While I started wading through websites and search engines, Diz put my cat down in a rare spot of sunshine that just happened to be shining on the comfiest part of the loveseat that takes up most of one wall in our front office. My cat settled in like the sun had decided to shine just for her. I should probably explain that when More-town Bay isn't fogged in, it's overcast. Or raining. Which explains why my hair tends more toward unmanageable frizz than cute brown curls.

Okay, so I might have a bit of Eros hair envy. I mean, it's just not fair when a guy's hair looks that good. Sure, Diz is gorgeous, but he's also got a mullet. A smooth, never-gets-frizzy, cinnamon-colored mullet with light streaks nearly the color of marshmallows, but it's still a mullet. That takes some of the sting out of getting my hairbrush stuck in a mess of tangles whenever I try to brush through the frizzy stuff.

After Diz got my cat settled on her loveseat throne, he took out his cell and started to make some phone calls. Diz was relatively young for an elf, but he'd been a police detective for a long time. Far longer than I had. He knew a lot of people, in and out of the department. If Dyte was anywhere out on the street, Diz's contacts would know.

Diz and I had been detectives with the Moretown Bay Police Department investigating magic-related crimes.

That assignment had been a serious stretch of my abilities. You see, for 99.9% of the time, I'm a plain old vanilla human. That other point one percent? Well, I have a touch of precognition.

Having a talent like that isn't as great as it sounds. I have absolutely zero control over it. My precog visions come and go as they please, which can be more annoying than helpful. The fact that I do have actual flashes of precognition had been enough for the top brass to assign a human woman to a detective squad sorely lacking in both.

I hoped that by doing a lot of research into Dyte and the Eros family business, I might give my talent a kick start, and in turn it would give me a flash to let me know where this runaway teenage god was hiding so we could go get her. Or, at the very least, we'd be able to find her and try to convince her to give her dad a call. I doubted even Diz, with all the strength and speed that went hand in hand with being an elf, could make a god do anything she didn't actually want to do.

It turned out that Eros had a very good reason for starting the search for his daughter in Moretown Bay, and it had nothing to do with the Oracle. Eros International, a division of CupidCo, Inc., had its west coast headquarters in the downtown financial district. I'd driven by the building more times than I could count and had no idea of its connection to one of the old gods. A steel and tinted-glass monstrosity, the building looked like the last place on earth you'd find a company that peddled the likeness of the chubby-cheeked god of love.

Eros said Dyte hadn't been seen or heard from in a week. I rather doubted that. Someone had to know where she was. Just because she wasn't actually at the office didn't mean her assistant didn't know how to find her. A good assistant always knew where the boss was. It was just a matter of persuading said assistant to spill the beans.

"I'm gonna go check something out," I said to Diz.

He had his cell phone about an inch away from his pointed ear. I'd tried to answer Diz's cell phone once, but he had the volume turned so low I couldn't hear a thing. Diz's ears were very sensitive. And intriguing. I had dreams about those pointy ears, all of which I had the good sense to keep to myself.

"Hang on," he said to whoever he was talking to. "Need company?" he asked me.

Diz was a grouch on his best days. That's why the department paired us up in the first place. No one wanted to work with Diz and his *mess with me and you die* personality, just like no veteran detective wanted to partner up with a human woman who had only marginal magical abilities at best and no control over them at worst. As it turned out, Diz and I got along pretty well while we were on the force. We still do. It helped that I thought his lack of elvish serenity was charming, in a perverse sort of way, and his mullet was kind of cute. I have no idea why he's still hanging around with me.

If I wanted to wheedle information out of Dyte's assistant, Diz wouldn't be much help.

"I got this one," I told him.

I could feel his eyes watching me as I headed out the door.

The afternoon sky was leaden grey with the kind of low clouds that only threatened rain if you carried an umbrella and drenched you in a sudden deluge if you didn't. I hated umbrellas, but I did have a hood on my coat. I tempted Fate by leaving the hood down.

My car was in the municipal lot, ten spaces away from the family in the van. I hunched my shoulders against the damp cold and tried not to trip myself up on the uneven sidewalk.

The masseuse had a new sign in her window. Valentine's Day Special: Full Body Massage, Two for One. Underneath, in smaller print, the sign read Masseuses Do It With A Friend. The sign featured hearts and arrows and a silhouette of baby Cupid with an arrow nocked in his bow.

The Asian market had Valentine's Day decorations in the windows. So did the bank the next block over. Even the coffee shop—not Starbucks—next to the bank was decorated for the holiday.

I'd never noticed all the decorations before. I've been single for a long time. In fact, my last boyfriend had broken up with me on February 12th. Instead of the romantic dinner for two I'd been hoping for, I ate take-out alone with my cat and a Love Stinks black and hot-pink toy skunk I'd bought to make myself feel better. It hadn't helped.

Valentine's Day put too much pressure on people. I'd never tell Eros this, but I agreed with Dyte. The day wasn't about celebrating love—it was about trying to live up to some impossible romantic ideal. It was one of those pseudo-holidays dreamed up by greeting card companies, like Boss's Day. I was pretty sure the world would be better off without it.

THE WEST COAST headquarters of Eros International was a madhouse.

I stepped off the world's fastest elevator onto the 14th floor of the tinted-glass and steel behemoth into something that looked more like an asylum where the patients had taken over rather than the corporate offices of an international conglomerate.

Okay, maybe it wasn't quite that bad, but it was close.

A pretty blonde receptionist, her hair in wild tendrils around her face, was trying to answer so many incoming calls that her "ErosInternationalpleasehold" came out in a single rushed word. A door in the paneled wall behind her was open and beyond was a fabric-covered cubicle wall. More phones beeped and twittered and jangled beyond that cubicle wall, and I could hear a rising babble of voices. The tension in those voices was unmistakable. As I watched the open door, a young man raced by, sheets of paper spilling from his over-loaded arms.

I stepped up to the reception desk and pasted a smile on my face. The receptionist gave me a *you've got to be kidding* look and kept answering her lines.

When I was on the force, all I'd have to do to get someone's attention was flash my badge. I didn't have a badge now. I went with my winning personality and cranked up the charm on my smile.

"I'm looking for Dyte," I said.

That was probably too familiar a way to refer to a corporate executive who happened to be a god, but I figured familiarity might get my foot in the door.

The receptionist paused for a split second in between calls. "She's not here."

"Any idea where she might be?"

She answered two more calls in quick succession. As far as I could tell, she wasn't actually transferring anyone, just putting the callers on hold. How many in-lines did this company have, anyway?

Instead of responding to my question, the receptionist made a quick *how the hell would I know?* gesture, rolled her eyes, and shrugged one shoulder.

"Can I speak to her assistant?" I asked.

Apparently I'd gone too far. The receptionist turned her complete attention back to her phones.

So much for the charm. I'd just have to ask someone else. The door to the inner sanctum was open, after all. That looked like an invitation to me.

Two steps inside, I almost got bowled over by a middle-management type. The man had a receding hairline, bifocals, and a well-worn suit coat. His tie was loose, and the top button on his white shirt was unbuttoned. He had an even bigger stack of papers in his hand than the guy I'd seen before. He dropped most of them on the floor when he crashed into me.

After I recovered my balance, I bent down to help him pick up his paperwork. Half of what I handed him were faxes, the rest spreadsheets. I didn't have time to read much, but the message on one fax was pretty clear: "Cancel My Order!" written in big block letters.

"What's going on here?" I asked Mr. Harried Middle Management.

"A disaster, it's all a disaster." He didn't look at me. He was shuffling papers, trying to collate his paperwork at light speed.

"What's a disaster?"

He squinted at me through the top part of his glasses. "You're not Quality Control, are you?" The way he said it, "Quality Control" sounded just this side of Satan.

"No." He didn't look like he believed me. "Trust me," I said. "I'm about the furthest thing from Q.C. as you can get."

"Good." He went back to scrambling after his paperwork. "She's going to be so upset with us."

"Dyte?"

"Yes! All these cancellations, right before the big day. It's our busy season. Like Christmas shopping is to mall stores. We make ninety percent of our annual sales in the three weeks before the Big Day, and now everyone's returning everything!"

Eros had only told me about licensing contracts. He didn't say anything about the fact that his company actually manufactured Valentine's Day products.

"What's being returned?" I asked.

"Everything!" He picked up one fax. "Chocolate hearts, the big boxes, are coming back by the truckload. The chocolate tastes bad." He shook the fax. "How can chocolate taste bad?" He showed me another fax. "Then there are the stuffed bears." He read from the fax through the bottom part of his glasses. "'The stuffing has the distinct odor of rotten eggs.'" He pushed his glasses up higher on his nose. "Rotten eggs! And that's just the beginning!"

I handed him the stack of papers I'd picked up.

"We were doing so well, too. Our biggest season ever. We'd even introduced a new line of dolls—Romance Through the Ages—they tested off the charts."

"And now?" I asked.

He picked up the last of the papers and stood up. "Canceled. The hair all frizzes."

Bad-tasting chocolate, stinky stuffed toys, and frizzy hair. And here I thought my Valentine's Days sucked.

"Any idea where Dyte might be?" I asked.

"No, and I don't want to know. She'd be so disappointed to see that we can't run things when she's gone." He gave me one more harried look. "And believe me, you don't want to disappoint this boss."

No kidding. Not if Dyte could reduce this poor man to a quivering nervous wreck. No job was worth that kind of stress.

Note to self—never, ever work for a teenage goddess.

～

Diz had no better luck with his street contacts than I'd had at Eros International.

"She probably skipped town," he said. "She's a god, she can do whatever she wants."

"Maybe not. Eros said even the gods have to play by the rules."

I was sitting on the little loveseat in our front office, in the same spot my cat had occupied earlier. Luckily, her long-hair grey tabby fur seems to blend in with my clothes. Either that or most people I meet are too polite to tell me that the seat of my jeans is covered in cat fur.

"That's what he told you?" Diz snorted. "The gods police themselves when it comes to their dealings with each other. But with the rest of us?"

I knew what he meant. Mythology books were chock full of stories about gods messing with other beings, most often us mere mortals, just for grins and giggles.

"I don't think that's what she's doing," I said. "This feels more like a temper tantrum. Daddy wouldn't give her what she wanted, so she's making it happen on her own. The net effect is the same."

"Cupid loses business."

"Eros. He prefers Eros."

Diz glowered, and I smiled. Yeah. No matter what Eros called himself, he was still the cherub-faced god who went around messing with people's love lives.

Across the street, a young couple stopped in front of the masseuse's shop. I watched them read her Valentine's Day sign. He was about twenty, bottle-black hair doing its best to stay spiky in the drizzling rain. He was holding hands with another boy the same age, thin as a rail with scraggly facial hair that might turn out to be a beard someday when it grew up. They looked at each other, grinned and nodded, and went inside for their two-for-one massage.

Even without the chocolates, the stuffed animals, the flowers and fancy dinners and jewelry, love found a way.

I sighed, leaned my head against the back of the loveseat...

...and promptly fell into one of the clearest precog visions I've ever had.

* * *

My visions aren't exactly private little mini-movies of the future screened inside my brain. Most of the time I see bits and pieces of things. A flashbulb-quick vision of a face. A whiff of a smell. A shiver of emotion. When the vision is intense, I taste things—bitter coffee, even more bitter bile, or sometimes even the coppery taste of blood. Gross.

This time around, I not only got the whole little mini-movie experience, I was *in* the movie. *Sleepless in Seattle*, to be precise.

I wasn't Meg Ryan's character and I wasn't Tom Hanks' or his son's. I was a guard at the Empire State Building. I could smell the cold, smoggy city air of New York. I felt the guard's tired feet, his stiff back, and the itchy scratch of the collar of his wool uniform coat. I ached with him as he watched Meg Ryan face the empty observation deck, knowing she was too late.

No, wait...

I wasn't the guard. I was someone who identified with the guard. Someone who felt like an outsider. Who watched other people fall in love, who helped other people fall in love, and couldn't find love herself.

I was Dyte, and she was about to watch this part of the movie.

I can't direct my precog visions; they don't work that way. Still, I tried to get a sense of where she was. It didn't seem like a private place. When I listened hard, I could hear the subtle rustling of clothes. Someone sniffled, someone else blew their nose quietly. I could see nothing but the movie, but there was a smell. I concentrated on that. Burnt and buttery. My mouth began to water. I hadn't had movie popcorn in a long time.

The vision faded, and in its place Diz's face hovered over me. I'd slipped down boneless on the little sofa. Diz had seen me have enough of these things that he didn't interfere, but his expression gave away his concern.

"Hey," I said, sitting up.

"Welcome back." He backed away to give me some space. "You okay?"

"Yeah, but I need a newspaper. I need to see the movie listings."

He blinked at me. "You want to go to a movie?"

"Yup." I grinned at him. "Dyte's a *Sleepless in Seattle* fan."

We missed Dyte at the theater. The movie was part of a Tom Hanks retrospective at a little independent theater nestled in between a Thai restaurant and a dry cleaners twenty minutes away from the office. By the time we got there, *Joe Versus the Volcano* had started. The theater was almost empty.

Great. I didn't think Eros would want to know that we'd missed his daughter by only a few minutes. Why couldn't my special talent be teleportation?

"What part of the movie was she watching?" Diz asked me.

We were standing outside the theater. The sun was going down, hidden by a tall office building across the street. There'd been a break in the clouds to the west, and the setting sun gave the buildings a soft, peachy-golden glow, but the air definitely had a chilly edge to it.

"The part on the Empire State building," I said. "Why?"

Diz pointed to the building across the street. It wasn't a tinted-glass and steel monstrosity. Made of gray stone masonry with tall arched windows, the building was only six stories tall. Elaborate stonework served as both a decoration and railing for a widow's walk that circled the building around a narrower top story.

"What does that remind you of?" he asked.

It wasn't quite the Empire State building, but it was close and convenient. "You think she's up there?"

He smiled at me. "One way to find out."

Oh, no.

"It'll only take a minute," Diz said.

This was such a bad idea. "This is such a bad idea," I said out loud.

Too late. Diz had already jogged across the street and was looking for a toe hold on the arch above a first floor window.

Diz doesn't exactly walk up walls. He doesn't exactly climb them either. He says it's an elf thing. I tell him people—and elves—aren't meant to walk vertically. He's never listened to me.

I watched from the sidewalk as he leapt from one toe and handhold to the next, essentially scaling the old building without benefit of rope or all that rock-climbing safety equipment I could never remember the names of. I felt like closing my eyes, at the same time I couldn't take my eyes off him.

We weren't cops anymore. We weren't supposed to take crazy chances like this. Of course, with an elf it wasn't as crazy a chance as it would be for me. He healed faster than I did, but I had no desire to find out whether an elf with a broken neck could heal himself or if the injury would kill him.

The longest minute of my life later, Diz finally reached the widow's walk. He vaulted over the edge and disappeared.

I stood on the sidewalk waiting. I couldn't get up to the roof the old-fashioned way. The front door was locked.

I waited some more. If Dyte wasn't up there, Diz should be back by now.

I'd been pacing for about five minutes when the front door opened and Diz stepped out.

I arched an eyebrow at him. "You picked the lock?"

"It's an elf thing."

Oh, goody. One more for the list. I'm going to have to start numbering all these "elf things" just to keep track.

Diz gestured with his head at the roof. "She wants to talk to you."

DYTE LOOKED like any other seventeen-year-old girl who thought being a Goth might be kind of cool, but not in a permanent tattoo and body-piercing way.

Her clothes were black, her nail polish was black, her hair was so black it was almost blue. She had a light, creamy complexion that managed to look healthy in spite of the lack of color. Her eyes were heavily lined in black, and she might have been wearing deep red lipstick at one time. Now the lipstick was smudged and half worn off, and the eyeliner had streaked down her cheeks.

She was leaning on her elbows on the decorative railing, an unlit cigarette in her hand. She was looking out over the city at the setting sun, but I figured she knew I was here.

"Hey," I said when I stepped out on the widow's walk.

She glanced at me and sniffled. "You piggybacked on me while I was at the movies."

She was talking about my vision. "You felt that?"

Dyte shrugged. "God, remember?" she said, pointing at herself. "I can pretty much feel everything if I want to."

Oh. That was interesting to know. Interesting and a little freaky.

I decided to let the freaky go for now. I could obsess about that later.

"So you knew I was looking for you."

"Yeah." She stared at the cigarette. "Dad says these aren't good for me. I can't see why. It's not like I'm ever going to get sick unless one of Dad's cronies decides to poison me. Or cast a spell on me. I think he's worried about his image. Smoking's not good for business."

She dropped the cigarette on the concrete floor of the widow's walk and crushed it beneath her black boot heel, even though the thing wasn't lit.

"Diz said you wanted to talk to me," I said.

"Yeah." She turned now and faced me fully. Even in the waning light, I could see how pretty she was. She had Eros's round angelic face, but with a bit more angle to her cheekbones. "What did Dad tell you about me?"

"That you have a good head for business."

"No, about why I left."

"He said you wanted him to cancel the licensing agreements for the right to his image."

She snorted.

48

"That wasn't exactly it, was it?" I asked, but I wasn't surprised. Clients never tell us the whole truth.

She nudged the crushed cigarette with the toe of her boot. "It's really hard having the God of Love for a dad. People get the wrong idea."

Not just people. If it was just about people, she wouldn't have been watching *Sleepless in Seattle*, a movie about soul mates and second chances.

"Guys," I said. "Guys get the wrong idea."

"Yeah." She pushed the cigarette around, leaving a streak of shredded paper and tobacco on the rough concrete. "They either think you're a slut or that your dad'll smite them if they even think about touching you."

"A guy who doesn't think either of those things would be pretty special, then."

Her eyes welled up and the corners of her mouth turned down. "Yeah," she said softly.

I had a pretty good idea what must have happened. Dyte fell for a boy, and Daddy didn't approve.

"What's his name?" I asked.

"Christopher. His name's Christopher." She wiped at her eyes with the back of her hand. More black eyeliner streaked out from the corners of her eyes. "He's the greatest guy I know. He's cute and sexy, and he didn't care who my dad was or what I was."

"Human?"

She nodded. "We were getting along so well, too, so I took him home to meet my parents. That's what girls do with guys they really like, right?"

She wasn't asking me, just telling her story, but I nodded anyway just in case.

"I mean, just because he was human shouldn't have been such a big deal. Mom used to be human, and Dad still fell in love with her. They got to get married and Mom became a god and gets to live with Dad forever, so why can't I? It's so unfair."

It hadn't escaped me that she was up here all alone and Christopher was nowhere to be seen. "Where is he?" I asked.

She shrugged. "He got scared. Daddy yelled at him. Daddy's got these special arrows. You know about them? He's not always just the God of Love. Sometimes he... he can make people fall out of love."

Eros really wouldn't have done that to the boy his daughter loved, would he?

Who was I kidding? He was a god. Messing with humans was in his job description.

"Did he shoot Christopher with one of those special arrows?"

"No." The word was small and made her sound about five years old. "He just... after he talked to Daddy, Christopher told me he didn't want to hate me someday, so he said he didn't want to see me anymore."

She didn't quite cry, but it was close. I got the feeling that she'd already cried herself out.

"Then you got mad," I said.

"Daddy's such a hypocrite. All this love, love, love stuff, and to think I bought it. I actually thought he was a good guy, but he's like everyone else—just out to make money any way he can. Do you know that he agreed to let someone use his image on toilet paper? Toilet paper?"

I thought I'd actually seen some of that in the novelty section of the Asian market.

"So you got even by tampering with the products," I said.

She nodded. "It was actually pretty easy to mess everything up. Way easier than keeping it going like it's supposed to."

Eros didn't need a detective. He needed a family counselor.

"If you got to choose," I said slowly, "what would you want?"

Her answer was immediate. "Christopher."

That wasn't going to happen, not if Christopher had truly flown the coop. "Besides Christopher," I said. "What do you want?"

She sighed. "If I can't have Christopher…"

I was pretty sure the reality of her first seriously broken heart had begun to settle in before I stepped out on the roof, but I still felt like a jerk for making her say it out loud. What was that about acceptance being the last stage of grief? Acceptance sucked.

"I just can't work in Dad's business anymore," she finally said. "I don't believe in it. So I guess what I really want is for him to fire me."

Now, this was something I'd never thought I'd see: Eros, the god of love; Dyte, his rebellious daughter; and Diz, my terminally grouchy partner, all seated in my office. Dyte and Eros sat in the chairs in front of my desk. Diz was glowering on the couch.

"As I see it," I said to the gods in my client chairs, "what we have here is a business opportunity in the making."

Eros's wings rustled beneath his suit, today a smartly cut dove grey. "If you're angling for a bonus, you won't get one. You found my daughter. That's the end of your services."

Dyte shot him a glare that rivaled one of Diz's. I was impressed.

"No bonus," I said. "This is on the house."

Diz glanced at me, one slightly raised eyebrow betraying his surprise, but I was feeling magnanimous.

"You managed to frighten away the love of your daughter's life," I said to Eros.

"There will be others," he said.

"Not hardly, not with you around," Dyte said under her breath. I was pretty sure that was for effect. If I could hear it, I knew everyone else in the room could hear it, too, especially her father.

I ignored Dyte and kept looking at Eros. "In exchange, I think you need to give Dyte something of value."

"She already runs my business office here."

"Something of value to *her*."

"Do I need to remind you that I do have arrows at my disposal?" Eros said.

Diz shifted on the couch. If looks could kill, Eros would have been a big pile of cinders.

I sat quietly in my chair and waited. I'm good at waiting. Stakeouts teach you that.

"What does she want?" Eros asked finally.

"My own company," Dyte said. "I don't want to work for you anymore."

I wondered if anything in Eros's long life had shocked him quite so much. He stared at his daughter, his mouth open in a little O. "You want me to just give you a company and walk away?"

"Yes."

I had to hand it to her. She stared him down, god to god, without throwing a temper tantrum, and with totally dry eyes and a calm expression to boot. A broken heart had apparently gone a long way toward making Dyte grow up.

"And just what would you do with that company?" Eros asked.

Dyte glanced at me. I reached beneath my desk and brought up the little black and hot-pink Love Stinks toy skunk. "There's a pretty big market in anti-Valentine's Day merchandise," I said. "I think this little guy's kinda cute, don't you?"

There for a minute I thought Eros's wings were going to break through his suit. "You want me to set up my daughter in direct competition with me?" He bit off every word as if he could barely stand to say them.

"Yes," I said calmly, putting the skunk on my desk. "And may the best god win."

~

A box of chocolates was on my desk first thing in the morning on February 14th.

I checked around in all the dark corners for a ticked off God of Love, but I didn't see Eros anywhere. What I did see was a certain self-satisfied elf curled up on the couch.

"Happy Valentine's Day," Diz said.

He was smiling.

"Turn around," I said. "I want to see if there's an arrow sticking out of your back."

He laughed. Diz didn't laugh often. Hearing his laughter was like popping the cork on a bottle of Dom Perignon. I considered pinching myself to see if I was still upstairs dreaming and what I thought was Diz's laughter was really my cat's snores.

"Seriously, though," I said. "What's the occasion?" It couldn't be what I thought it might. Could it?

He unfolded himself from the couch. "Do you realize that you went up against one of the old gods and won?"

Yeah, that hadn't escaped me. I kept waiting for the snick and whoosh and thump of an arrow in my back, but so far... nothing. Maybe Psyche had convinced her husband it was all for the best.

"Well, Eros is going to figure out sooner or later that

his family's cornered both sides of the Valentine's Day market," I said.

The box of chocolates was shaped like a huge cartoon heart and wrapped in red cellophane. I wondered how much candy I'd scarf down before I'd have to hide the thing somewhere. I never could get myself to throw out chocolate. It seemed almost sacrilegious.

I had a sudden thought. "This box didn't come from Eros International, did it?"

"Why?"

I remembered what Mr. Harried Middle Management had said about their customer complaints. The chocolate tasted bad.

"Well..." I scrunched up my nose. How to tell my partner that his thoughtful present might not be such a great idea after all?

Misdirection. If I didn't mention it, he'd never know.

"I have an idea," I said. I turned him around so that we were both facing the masseuse's shop across the street. "She's still having a special. Two for one. How about we go celebrate the successful resolution of the Eros family crisis with a cut-rate massage?"

Diz's eyebrows practically climbed off his forehead. "You're kidding."

"Nope!" Okay, maybe I was a little, but hey, my grouchy partner just gave me a box of chocolates for Valentine's Day. If that wasn't an omen to push the boundaries of our partnership a little bit, I didn't know what was.

Diz gave me a good long look. I don't know what he

saw in my expression, but he didn't growl at me. Instead, he switched the little neon *Open* sign in our front window off and held the door open for me.

Wow. He was actually taking me up on my off-the-wall invitation.

I let out a little pent-up breath. I was about to get a massage with my hunky elf partner. I couldn't wait to see what he looked like wearing nothing but a towel.

Happy Valentine's Day to me!

JUST MY LUCK

I'd just kicked back in my chair with my feet up on my desk, the first cup of coffee of the morning steaming a wonderful, fresh-brewed aroma, when a snazzy little man in a kelly-green suit opened the door to my office.

When I say little, I mean this guy was little. No more than three feet tall, he was perfectly proportioned, from tiny feet encased in black leather loafers to the top of his wee curly-haired head. He had chubby cheeks and coppery-red hair, and a full beard to match. Brilliant green eyes peered out at me from behind gold-rimmed, rectangular spectacles.

He shut the door firmly behind him then turned to face me. He held a green fedora that matched his suit in hands that looked far stronger than their diminutive size implied.

"I'm wondering," he said, his voice surprisingly deep

for someone so small. "Do you think you can help me, miss? I've come about someone gone missing."

That's what I do. I help people find other people. I'm Dee, one half of D & D Investigations, and as the sign says on the glass window in the front office, Missing Persons Are Our Specialty.

However, just because someone's polite enough to call me "Miss" doesn't mean I'm a pushover.

I dropped my feet on the floor, sat up straight, and narrowed my eyes at my potential client. Except for his size and his red hair, this guy bore more than a passing resemblance to Cupid... er, Eros. I'd already helped one member of the God of Love's huge family, and instead of a "thank you" for my trouble, I got a box of bad-tasting Valentine's Day chocolates and a tantalizing yet all too brief glimpse of my partner's towel-clad physique.

"You're not related to Eros, are you?" I asked.

The little man blinked. "Not that I'm aware of."

"And you're not an elf?"

He blinked again. "No."

Don't get me wrong. I have nothing against elves. My partner's an elf. A tall one. Diz, the other half of D & D, is built like The Rock back when The Rock was still The Rock and not Dwayne Johnson, movie star. Trust me. I've seen nearly all of Diz, and when I say he's built, he's *really* built. Diz also has The Rock's glower, without the raised eyebrow thing The Rock used to do, and about as much patience as I can fit in the tip of my little finger. But Diz and I had a whole passel of dinky little elves for clients right before Christmas, and let me tell you, I'd give just about anything for a normal client right about now.

Not that I was going to get it.

"I'm a leprechaun," the little man said.

Now it was my turn to blink.

"Seriously?" I almost dropped my coffee. "Aren't you afraid to tell people that? I mean, if I capture you, don't you have to grant me three wishes?"

The little man sighed and rolled his eyes behind his gold-rimmed glasses. "Stereotypes," he said.

"You are wearing green."

"The color goes well with my beard."

"I guess that means you don't have a pot of gold at the end of the rainbow." Too bad. Diz and I weren't exactly up to our armpits in paying work at the moment.

"If I did, do you think I'd be looking for a detective in this neighborhood?"

True. Diz and I can't afford a swanky office in one of Moretown Bay's uptown high-rises. Instead, our office is in a neighborhood where the cracked sidewalk looks like half-deflated accordion pleats and the municipal parking lot down the block houses at least one family in an old panel van. Not that we don't have good neighbors. I know from personal experience that the masseuse across the street gives a heck of a backrub, and the woman who runs the Asian store next door sells the most scrumptious lychee jellies I've ever tasted.

"Okay," I said. "Fair enough." I was about to offer him a seat, but the two client chairs in front of my desk weren't exactly leprechaun sized. Neither was the

ANNIE REED

loveseat against the side wall. If we kept getting pint-sized clients, we'd really have to do something about that. "Why don't you tell me who's missing?"

He eyed the client chairs, the loveseat, and then looked at me sitting in my comfortable old executive chair behind my desk. He made a grumpy little noise, and before I knew it, he'd hopped up into one of the chairs faster than I could have gotten out of mine.

"How'd you do that?" I asked.

"Leprechaun," he said. "We are a type of fairy, you know."

Huh. As a general rule, fairies tended not to get along well with elves.

"In the interests of full disclosure, then," I said. "I should tell you that I'm only one half of D & D Investigations. My partner is an elf."

The little man's eyes grew wide. "An elf? Oh, my, that will never do." He worried the brim of his hat with his hands. "Not do at all. Would I be hiring the both of you, or could my business be strictly with you?"

I had to think about that. Diz and I had been partners for years, starting back when we were both cops in the Bureau of Magical Enforcement of the Moretown Bay Police Department. Diz got stuck with me because no one else would put up with his bad disposition, and I got stuck with Diz because no one else wanted to partner with a human woman whose only qualification for the magical side of police work was a smidgen of precognition that kicked in whenever it damn well felt like it. We made the partnership work, even after we

60

both left the cops and opened a private detective agency.

I'd never investigated a case without Diz before, but we could really use the money. We were late on this month's rent, and considering that I lived in the apartment upstairs, I didn't want to lose both my office and my home. Diz lived in a one-bedroom apartment close to the touristy section of the city near the waterfront. While I might harbor certain non-work related fantasies about my grumpy partner—say for instance, a particular favorite in which I ran a finger around the tip of his pointy ears—I didn't think our friendship, much less our partnership, would survive if I had to move myself and my cat into Diz's apartment.

Luckily for my potential client, Diz had sent me a text earlier that morning to let me know he'd be otherwise occupied this morning. It's an elf thing, he'd said. I kept an ever-growing mental list of elf things. I planned to get even by starting my own list of it's a human thing one of these days.

"Why don't you tell me a little about what you'd like to me do?" I said. "It will be strictly between the two of us, even if I don't take the case."

The little man relaxed into the chair. "That would do just fine."

He introduced himself as Seamus Flannery. The person who was missing was his business partner. "Katie Kennan," he said. "We've been in business together in this fair town for nearly forty years, Katie and I."

Flannery didn't look nearly that old, but one thing I

did know about fairies is that, like most magical folk, they lived far longer than vanilla mortals like me.

"What business?" I asked.

He sighed. "We make shoes."

I raised both eyebrows. "Are you sure you don't have a pot of gold at the end of the rainbow?"

He shrugged. "The legends, they do come from somewhere."

Of course, they do, and legends about leprechauns said they spent their time making shoes, playing practical tricks, and hoarding their gold. It made me wonder what else the legends were right about.

"Katie and I," Flannery said, "we started out making fine gentlemen's shoes, but the money these days comes from athletics." His eyes twinkled. "I do believe that the shoes you're wearing came from one of our discount shops."

My tennis shoes? I loved the things, and I could have cared less that they came from a strip mall discount store. Wearing what I wanted to work was one of the best perks of owning your own business. True, as a detective I hadn't been forced to wear a street cop's uniform. Still, the department had frowned on jeans and hoodies.

But if Flannery was not only a shoemaker but also owned a bunch of discount shoe stores, didn't that mean he was wealthier than he let on? "I thought you said you didn't have a lot of money," I said.

"Ah, now, as I remember, you asked if I had a pot o'

gold. Are we going to be spending our time discussing such silly legends when my poor Katie is missing?"

Point taken. "Tell me what you know," I said.

Flannery told me he and Katie ran their business out of a warehouse on the south side of the Moretown Bay, which the city creatively referred to as South Bay. They had a small staff who handled the automated end of shoe production and delivery, and the retail stores were all run as franchise outlets. Flannery and Katie spent their time working on design and development. "The modern day equivalent of cobbling together bits of leather into fine footwear," Flannery said. "It's what makes us the happiest."

Or it did until three days ago when Katie didn't come to work.

"I tried to reach her," Flannery said, "but she wouldn't answer her phone."

Two days ago, one of the machines in the production office malfunctioned and had to be shut down. Replacement parts were on back order.

Yesterday, two of his franchise owners notified Flannery that they weren't going to renew their contracts.

This morning, his production foreman quit.

"You've had quite the run of bad luck," I said.

"It's Katie." Flannery's mouth turned down at the corners, and the twinkle left his eyes. "She's my lucky charm, if you pardon the expression. I was a simple shoe maker until she came into my life. She was the ambitious one, you see. Leprechauns aren't social by nature. I was quite content to cobble shoes together here and there. That's how I met my Katie. She came to me for a pair of shoes for a wedding, and she said they were the best fit she'd ever had. I ended up making shoes for the whole wedding party."

I didn't miss that this wasn't the first time he'd called her "my Katie."

"Have you been to the police?" I asked. "Filed a missing persons report?"

"With an officious little dwarf whose name I can't remember, he made me so upset." Flannery shook his head. "I've no evidence of foul play, I believe he called it, so the 'report is on file.'"

I knew any number of bad-tempered dwarves who were desk sergeants. They were the kind of cops who gave dwarves a bad name.

"Is it possible she simply took a vacation? A trip? Forgot to tell you, or sent you an email that didn't make it?" Lord knows, I've accidentally deleted the wrong emails or failed to send the right ones.

"That's not like my Katie," Flannery said. "She wouldn't leave without saying goodbye."

There was that "my Katie" again.

I leaned forward and put on my best understanding expression. "She's not just your business partner, is she?"

Behind his gold-rimmed spectacles, Flannery's eyes got shiny bright, and his chubby cheeks sagged. "No," he said. "She's the light of my life, my girl is." He looked down at the hat he still clutched in his hands. "I don't know what I'll do if she's really gone."

It took a bit of work to keep my own eyes from

turning shiny bright. I understood how the little man felt. I wouldn't know what to do if Diz ever left me. Okay, so I'd never call him my Diz, but I was attached just the same. I'd come to think of my partner as my partner for life. Even if I never got to run my finger along his pointy ears and see if it had the same effect on him in real life that it had in my fantasies, I seriously expected to spend the foreseeable future with His Grumpiness.

"Okay," I said. "I'll take your case. I have to tell you though, since Katie's an adult, if I find her and she doesn't want to come back, I can't do anything to force her to come back. I'll only be able to tell you she's all right. Will you be good with that?"

Flannery nodded.

"Do you have a picture of her?"

He shook his head. "No. She's not one for pictures, you know?"

Okay, that made things a little harder, but with luck, I might be able to track down a picture of her on the Internet. If she'd been in business with Flannery in Moretown Bay for forty years, there was bound to be a photograph of her somewhere.

I had Flannery sign our standard retainer contract. He paid one day's fees in advance with regular old cash, not with pieces of gold—although that would have been neat—and left me with Katie's address, the company's address, and his cell phone number. I wondered if he kept his cell in a kelly-green case.

After Flannery left, I pulled out my own cell phone.

Time to tell my partner I was going to be occupied for the day. Without him.

I sighed as I typed in the text. I was going to miss him. I told myself it would be good for me to take a day at work away from Diz. Just in case.

Oh, good grief. I was borrowing trouble, as my mom used to say. I'd better find Seamus Flannery's Katie soon, or I'd end up with a serious case of the clings next time I saw my partner, not that he'd never let me get away with that.

To make myself feel better, right before I hit send, I typed in four more words: It's a human thing.

Let him figure that one out.

Most of our investigations start the same way. I get on the Internet and see what I can dig up, and Diz makes a few calls. He has more street contacts than I ever had. He was the "bully and intimidate" part of our good cop/insane cop interrogation team back when we'd been detectives. Diz's street connections continue to supply him with information even though he's no longer a cop just to stay on his good side. Even without Diz around to make the phone calls, I figured my best bet was still the Internet.

Before I started to research Katie Kennan, I spent some time digging up background on my client. If I've learned nothing else in the detective biz, it's that clients lie. Oh, they don't usually mean to lie. They just leave a little information out because they don't think it's important, or they might twist the truth a quarter turn away from center to make themselves look better. It helps if I know going in how much I can trust the person footing the bill.

Besides, leprechauns had a reputation as practical jokers. Not that I could envision Seamus Flannery kicking up his heels and spinning on the top of that kelly-green hat of his, cackling about what a good one he pulled over on that gullible vanilla mortal who ran her own detective agency. Still, it didn't hurt to be informed.

I found out that Flannery had told me the truth, as far as it went. He was one of two corporate officers for Cobblers, Incorporated, a business founded forty-one years ago. The other named officer was Kathryn Kennan. The corporation owned the warehouse in South Bay at the address Flannery had given me. Cobblers, Incorporated, was a privately owned corporation, not publicly traded. I could have found out what the company's net worth was with a little not-strictly-legal digging, but unless I discovered that Katie was being held for ransom, I didn't think going that far into Flannery's financial background was necessary.

The brand name of my tennis shoes was Cobbler-stones. The franchise stores were also known as Cobbler-stones, and there were seven in the greater Moretown Bay area. The store I shopped at was the closest, just a few blocks away from the office in an area the city was trying to reclaim from decay and recreate as a destination outlet store outdoor mall. Flannery hadn't said if the

Cobblerstones I shopped at was one of the two stores the franchise holder was giving back to the company, but a simple visit should answer that question. After all, I wasn't just a detective, I was a repeat customer. That should count for something.

What I did discover, quite by accident, wasn't quite a lie. Flannery had told me that Katie didn't like to have her picture taken, which was probably true, although the way he'd said it implied that, like a lot of women, Katie had a love/hate relationship with how she saw herself versus what she really looked like. In the city's historical society records, which the city had just completed putting online, I found an old newspaper story, complete with grainy photograph, about the opening of the first Cobblerstones franchise thirty-five years ago. In the photo, Flannery stood in front of the store, which was down in the area of town close to where Diz lived. Next to Flannery stood a man and woman, apparently human. All three were beaming wide smiles at the photographer. Flannery looked about the same as he had today in my office. Damn those fairy genes. Elves and fairies never had to worry about the beginnings of crow's feet at the corners of their eyes.

I assumed the man and woman in the photograph were husband and wife. The tiny print below the photograph was impossible to read, so there was no reason for me to believe otherwise.

At least there wasn't until I found a photograph of the outlet mall store's opening day ceremonies ten years ago. There was that same woman again, this time standing next to Flannery. I had no trouble reading the print for this article.

Flannery had run the store himself when it first opened. They both had, Flannery along with his Katie, who stood a good two feet taller than Flannery.

She wasn't a leprechaun. And if the photographs were anything to go by, she wasn't exactly human either, because during the twenty-five years between photographs, it didn't look like she'd aged a day.

MORETOWN BAY IS the home to any number of magical folk who don't age like humans do. Elves like Diz age so slowly they're nearly immortal. Diz is pretty young as elves go. His full name is Dizzy G, named for the jazz great Dizzy Gillespie by Diz's music-loving mother. Not that a lot of people know my grumpy partner's full name. Dwarves live to a ripe old age, too, and so do changelings. Not to mention fairies of the leprechaun and non-leprechaun variety. Goblins can wear human faces when they want to, which is not often, although goblins rarely engage in any kind of business that doesn't involve some sort of criminal activity. At least, not in my experience.

Katie Kennan could have been any one of those long-lived non-humans, or she could simply be a non-leprechaun fairy. It still made me wonder why she'd hang out with Flannery for forty years and then up and disappear one day. The fact that she wasn't a leprechaun was a big fact that Flannery had left out of his tale, but then again, I'd never asked, just assumed. And yes, I know the saying. I just need to be slapped upside the head with it every now and then so that I remember to ask even the things that might seem to be rude.

I printed out the photograph of the opening day of the Cobblerstones shoe store in the discount strip mall, grabbed my raincoat, and took off for the mall. It was one of those weird-weather days in Moretown Bay, the kind that can't make up its mind whether it's going to rain, the sun's going to shine, or fog's going to roll in off the bay before dark. I've taken to wearing my raincoat, complete with hood, as a matter of course. My hair frizzes in the best of times. I've learned to live with the frizz, but I don't do the drowned-rat look well at all.

While I walked, I took the time to check in with Diz. We might each be doing our own thing today, but that didn't mean we couldn't stay in touch.

Except I just got his voicemail, which was short and to the point.

"You know who you called. Leave a message."

That was my grumpy partner, all right.

"Hey, yourself," I said into the phone. "I'm on my way out to do a little digging. I'll check in with you later. I thought you might like to do take-out for dinner." I paused, then added, "My cat misses you."

I winced at that last. My cat did have a thing for Diz. His shoulder was the only one she'd sleep on, and wonder of wonders, he let her. She had all the luck. And even though Diz did like Chinese take-out, I knew I was reaching.

"Okay, gotta go," I said in a rush before I pressed *end call* on my phone.

Sheesh. I have no idea why he puts up with me.

The rain started to fall in earnest right as I got to the shoe store. I ran the last few steps to the front door, not that it's ever been shown that running through the rain gets you less wet.

"Welcome to Cobblerstones!" said the clerk, a teenaged girl with round, black-rimmed glasses that gave her an owlish look. "Anything I can help you with?"

I'd never seen this clerk before. So much for having an "in" with the staff.

"Yeah," I said as I pushed the hood of my raincoat down. "Can you tell me if the owner's here today?"

The girl looked nervous. "The owner? You mean my boss?" She glanced at my wet feet. "Is there something wrong with your shoes?"

I smiled at her. "Relax," I said. "I love my shoes. I just need to ask your boss a few questions."

She heaved a visible sigh. "Oh. Okay. He's in the back. Give me a minute?"

"No problem."

I browsed the aisles while I waited. I'm not a shopa-holic, not nearly, but I do like a comfortable tennis shoe. Now that I knew the background of the shoemaker, I could see bits and pieces of what must have been his "fine gentlemen's" shoes in the design of these tennis shoes. Some of the models, if they'd been made of polished black leather, wouldn't have looked all that bad with the dress slacks I'd had to wear as a detective. Why hadn't I heard about Cobblerstones shoes back then? I could have saved myself many nights soaking my aching feet, especially back in the first few years I'd been a street cop and spent my days handing out parking tickets. With shoes like these, I could have pounded the pavement in comfort.

Or, I could have pounded the pavement with wet feet.

I was squelching with each step I took.

I looked down at my shoes. Water was leaking out of the seams along the soles. I had left a trail of Dee-sized shoeprints from the door all the way to where I stood.

It hadn't been that wet outside, had it?

"Can I help you?"

I looked up from my sopping-wet shoes to find a middle-aged man staring at me with a resigned look on his tired face. He didn't have a name tag on the pocket of his dress shirt. His sleeves were rolled halfway up his forearms, and his tie hung loose and crooked.

"My shoes are leaking," I said, surprising myself, but I guess I was still pretty shocked to be standing in a shoe store with wet socks.

The man sighed. "I'll be happy to refund your money or replace the shoes," he said. His flat tone told me I wasn't the first customer with this complaint.

"Thanks," I said.

"What size are you?"

I told him. He did a double-take. Okay, so my feet aren't tiny, but they're not clown-shoe sized either.

"I take after my dad," I said.

He didn't look like he believed me.

I followed the store owner down the aisle to my size. Luckily—or unluckily, seeing how fast these shoes had sprung a leak—they had the same style in stock.

I kicked off my leaky shoes and sat down on a stool to put the new shoes on. The owner took one look at my soaked socks and offered to throw in a new pair at half price.

"So, I guess this has happened a lot?" I asked the owner after the sales clerk went to retrieve the socks.

"For the last few weeks, yeah," the owner said. "I don't understand it, quality's always been a hallmark with the company, but I can't afford it anymore."

"Don't they reimburse you for damaged stock?"

He made a face. "They used to, but lately it's all about profits, profits, profits. I can't keep up."

I decided to play dumb. This guy was disgruntled enough to share his woes with a customer, and I wanted to keep him talking.

"Does this mean you're closing?" I asked. "I'd be sorry to hear it. I've been shopping here for years."

"Don't worry. The company'll take over the store after I'm gone. This used to be their most profitable location, you know, even with the one downtown raking in all the summer tourist trade. One season does not a year make. I'd like to see Kate the Terrible turn the kind of profit I have."

Kate the Terrible?

"Is that your boss?" I asked.

"One of them," he said. "I haven't seen Seamus in years. She probably has him tied up in a dungeon somewhere, cranking out new styles four times a year. Poor little guy."

Huh. Flannery had said his Katie was ambitious. He never mentioned ruthless. Although this guy's bitterness against her could just be a by-product of short-timer's syndrome combined with an unlucky run of defective products.

The teenage clerk came back with new socks. Dry socks. I peeled my wet ones off and shoved them in a pocket, and put the new ones on. I never knew dry socks could feel so good. The clerk smiled at me, and I wondered if she would still have a job after Cobblers Incorporated took the store back over. I hoped so.

"So what are you going to do?" I asked the owner once I had my new shoes laced up. "I've always been a happy shopper, and you obviously take care of your customers."

"Frozen yogurt shop," he said. "I'm opening a new franchise at the other end of the mall. A serve yourself place." He actually smiled. "Frozen yogurt's the new coffee."

I wondered if anyone had told Starbucks that.

I SPENT the rest of the morning visiting three more Cobblerstones shoe stores. This time I drove. I wanted to keep my new shoes leak-free as long as possible. Given Flannery's current run of bad luck, which I had no doubt encompassed all the discount mall store's leaky footwear, I wanted my feet to stay warm and dry as long as possible. Whether or not Cobblerstones were prone to spring leaks during rainy weather, they were still the most comfortable tennis shoes I'd ever worn.

Since I didn't have to pretend to be a customer returning a defective product, I told the other store owners that I was a private detective doing some background work in conjunction with confidential financial matters for the parent corporation. It must have sounded like a plausible enough reason to the franchise owners because none of them questioned my cover story.

Each of the owners—two men and one woman—had the same opinion of Katie Kennan as the first owner did, although none of them called her Kate the Terrible. At least, not in those words. The woman called her "that bitch from corporate." They all agreed that lately Katie had been pushing them to make greater and greater profits, of which Cobblers Incorporated got a healthy percentage.

"From your perspective, is the company in trouble?" I asked the woman manager, whose name was Maria Gossy. "Is that why they're pushing you for bigger profits?"

Maria wasn't entirely human. If I'd had to guess, I'd say she had dwarf blood swimming in her gene pool given her aggressiveness, not to mention her incredibly thick, long hair.

She snorted. "You're the detective, so detect. All I know is they keep wanting a bigger and bigger cut. I'm waiting for them to tell me we need to renegotiate the percentages in my contract. I've got a great contracts lawyer. He's a wizard. I can't wait to see that bitch's face when she figures that out."

I'd worked for wizards in the police department. No one wanted a full-fledged wizard on the other size of any argument. Wizards fought dirty, and they could get away with it.

I stood outside the last franchise shoe store and wondered what my next move should be. I was supposed to be finding a missing woman, and so far, all I'd dug up were a lot of bad feelings about her among the owners of franchise stores. I hadn't asked Flannery if Katie had any enemies. I was beginning to get the feeling that pretty much anyone she'd dealt with recently could be an enemy, and enemies didn't play fair. Had one of her employees had done more than bad talk the boss?

I really needed Diz. I was starting to get a bad feeling about this case. We weren't cops anymore. We didn't investigate crimes, and if one of Katie Kennan's enemies had decided to strike back at her, that was a crime. We reunited missing people with people who loved them. Or, like with Santa's elves, with the co-workers who needed them.

Except I couldn't call Diz. I'd promised Flannery I wouldn't involve my elf partner.

"You know, I could use a little help here," I muttered to my recalcitrant precog power. Not that I expected any help on that front. I never had any control over when and where a precog vision kicked in, but without Diz, the only advantage I had was my ability to see little glimpses of the future.

A sudden wave of dizziness made my head spin. I blinked to try to clear my head, but the sidewalk stayed tilted beneath my feet, and the rest of the real world around me started to fade away.

Well, what do you know.

For once, my precog power decided to show up right when I needed it.

I STARTED HAVING PRECOG "EPISODES," as my mother put it, right around the time I hit puberty. Didn't that turn out to be just the most fun time of my life, ever.

Since then, I've gotten used to having reality fade away on a somewhat irregular basis. I've learned to recognize the signs, and if I'm driving when a vision starts to hit, I pull off the road fast. Driving under the influence of precognition isn't a ticketable offense, at least not yet, but the last thing I want to do is hurt someone just because I can't see where I'm going.

Sometimes my precog visions are little more than flashbulb images that make about as much sense as viewing one still frame from each scene of a two-hour movie. I'll get glimpses of all the players and sometimes the place but understand none of the context. Other times, my vision gifts me with smells and the feel of a place but won't show me who's there. The best visions are like mini-movies in my head, complete with surround sound, 3D visuals, and Smell-O-Vision.

This precog episode wasn't a mini-movie. The vision hit me more like a frame-by-frame slideshow of a movie, except this one was a jittery old black-&-white silent.

I didn't understand what I was seeing at first. A hammer kept swinging through my field of vision to strike at something too out of focus to tell exactly what it was.

No, not a hammer. A mallet.

Swing. Bap! Swing. Bap! Swing. Bap!

I concentrated, but all I could see was the mallet and the hand that held it. Unhelpful in the extreme.

Or maybe not. I recognized that hand. Small, but stronger than its size implied.

The hand swinging the mallet belonged to Seamus Flannery.

As soon as I recognized the hand, that part of my vision flickered away, only to be replaced with the back of a head. A head sporting a cinnamon-colored mullet.

Have I mentioned that my partner has a mullet? No? Well, the haircut's not his best feature, but it does show off his pointy ears nicely.

In my vision, Diz was walking away from me down what looked like a long corridor, and he wasn't alone. A woman strolled next to him. A woman with pointy ears of her own.

And she had her hand tucked into the crook of my partner's arm!

Okay, vision, what the heck was this?

I had no time to get more than superficially upset about the idea of my partner strolling along with someone other than me before the vision changed yet again. This time I got the silent movie version of the touristy waterfront area of Moretown Bay. The streets really were cobbled down there, plus they were closed to all but pedestrian traffic. Tourists of all shapes, sizes, and species crowded the shops at all hours of the day. Some of the best fish in the city came from the open-air market, and pretty much anything else you wanted to legally buy could be found there.

My vision ended with a close-up of the logo of a store I'd seen often but never patronized. One minute I was right outside the store, staring up at the sign, and the next I was sitting on the sidewalk of Cobblerstones Discount Shoes, my back against the plate glass window and my legs splayed out in front of me, with the manager of the store standing over me, hands on her hips.

"Hey, you okay?" asked Maria Gossy. "What's wrong with you?"

Many things, I was sure, but nothing she needed to know about. "I'm fine," I said. "Thanks for all your help."

Not that she'd helped me, but it never hurt to be nice to someone who hadn't let some stranger steal my purse while I was temporarily out of it.

I got to my feet and hurried to my car. I knew where to go, thanks to my vision.

In a twisted sort of way, it all made sense. Where do you find a clue about the missing love of a leprechaun's life?

The Rainbow Condoms store. Where else?

THE LEPRECHAUNS of legend loved one thing above all else —gold. Stories go that the wee little shoemakers hid their gold in a pot buried at the end of the rainbow.

The only permanent rainbow in Moretown Bay was the logo for the Rainbow Condoms store.

I had no idea why Diz had been in my vision or who he'd been with, but I had no time to think about it. I drove as fast as I could through yet another downpour toward the waterfront tourist district. My visions didn't tend to be long-range things. Back when Diz and I helped Eros find his wayward daughter Dyte, my precog abilities had given me a vision of where she'd be but not enough time to get there before she left. Typical. Since my vision of Flannery with the mallet and Rainbow Condoms was the only decent clue I'd come up with in this case, other than the apparent fact that Katie Kennan was a money-grubbing, difficult-to-work-for, not-quite-human woman who'd somehow managed to capture a leprechaun's heart, I didn't want to get to the condom store only to learn that I'd arrived too late.

I needn't have worried. The Rainbow Condoms store was closed, an apparent victim of the recession.

What the heck?

My precog ability had never steered me so wrong.

I stood in the rain outside the locked door of the former condom store, regretting now that I'd never screwed up my courage enough to go inside. It might have been fun. I wondered if they'd sold glow-in-the-dark condoms, and for just a moment, I let myself wonder whether my partner could ever be convinced to wear one. Not that I'd likely find out first hand, but it was fun to think about.

The old condom store was the street-side, street-level shop in what looked like a series of smaller retail stores carved out of a much larger two-story building. Moretown Bay had quite a few places like that, especially in the waterfront area. The city encouraged former warehouses to convert into malls of a sort to attract the tourist dollar. If the condom store's mall was anything like the other former warehouse malls I'd been in, each of the shops inside would be tiny little stores, with corridors winding between them and creaky stairs leading to the second level. There might even be a lower level built into the hill behind the building. Like a lot of the waterfront property around the Bay, the land rose up steeply behind the Rainbow Condoms building. What was the second floor on the bay side might turn into the ground floor level at the back, so there might even be more than one basement level. I didn't have a clue. Not having been born with a shopping gene, I'd never browsed through this building before.

Maybe my vision had given me the one-of-a-kind landmark as a starting point, not the ultimate destination. Well, I was here. What could it hurt to go wandering inside and see what turned up? It was better than standing in the rain waiting for my new tennis shoes to spring a leak.

Once inside, I walked past an import clothing store, a marvelous-smelling deli that sold piroshkies, and the inevitable t-shirt shop. The floor in this part of the building was uneven, and my new shoes squeaked on linoleum. Good thing I wasn't trying to be stealth detective.

Or at least I wasn't until I turned down a side corridor and saw the back of my partner's head. He was heading in the same direction I was, two stores in front of me.

Diz is a tall elf. He's easy to spot, even for someone like me who's a little less than average height. Not that I'm leprechaun short, but the top of my head reaches the top of Diz's shoulder, if that. Still, I'd know that cinnamon-colored mullet anywhere.

The corridor wasn't too crowded, so I hung back and watched and tried to keep the green-eyed monster from taking over my brain.

Because there she was, the woman from my vision. She was walking next to Diz, and she had her hand in the crook of his elbow. I couldn't see her ears from this distance—I don't have elfen vision—but I would have bet those ears were perfectly pointed.

Who was she? Diz never mentioned whether or not he dated, not in all the years we'd known each other. I mean, he had to have dated, right? Even I'd had a few—

very few—boyfriends here and there, although I had a longer relationship with my cat than I'd had with any of the guys who'd come into and out of my life.

Part of me felt guilty following Diz and his mystery elf. Sure, I had fantasies about my gorgeous partner. What red-blooded woman wouldn't? That didn't mean I had any right to expect him to act on fantasies he didn't even know about. He had every right to blow off a day of working with me to spend it with someone he wanted to be with, right?

Right?

But if I wasn't supposed to watch them, then what the heck had my vision been about? It had clearly shown me Seamus Flannery swinging a mallet at something. I hadn't been able to see what he'd been hitting, but I guessed it must have been nails in the sole of a shoe.

Except...

My visions didn't show me things from the past. Flannery had said he worked in design and development these days and that shoe manufacturing was automated. Even if one of the manufacturing machines had broken down, like he'd told me that morning, he wouldn't have gone back to making shoes one mallet swing at a time. Would he?

But if he wasn't hand-crafting shoes, what then?

I kept my partner and the mystery woman in view as I tried to conjure up images from my vision. Gradually, I realized something I'd overlooked.

When I'd explained to myself what the vision had looked like, I'd described it as a silent movie, but that hadn't been quite right. Now that I seriously thought about it, I'd heard a clinking noise during the black and white slideshow. At the time I'd associated the noise with the sound an old-fashioned movie projector makes. What if it had been something else?

Like the sound of a mallet striking a chain.

Was that what I'd seen? Flannery using the mallet to try to break the metal links of a chain?

But that made no sense. Flannery had been in my office just that morning. Why would my vision show me Flannery trying to break chains? Sure, maybe Flannery was chained by his feelings for "his" Katie, but my visions didn't work in metaphors. Thank goodness. I already had a hard enough time trying to figure them out.

Up ahead, Diz stopped in front of a store. His companion turned to him and smiled, and now I could see the curve of her pointed ear.

Damn it.

She said something to him, then turned and headed toward the restrooms.

I nearly forgot to breathe. I couldn't have just seen what I thought I did. Could I?

The woman had faced me for a moment just before she turned down the corridor that led to the restrooms. She'd been out of Diz's line of sight for just an instant. In that instant, I hadn't seen her as the tall elf woman who'd been holding onto Diz's elbow.

In that instant, the woman had looked exactly like

the photograph of Katie Kennan folded up in the pocket of my jeans.

What the heck was going on here?

BACK WHEN DIZ and I had worked for the Police Department, we'd arrested more than our fair share of changelings.

Changelings were magical creatures who could be anyone at all provided they had some sample of the person they were copying to go by, whether that sample was a picture or a touch or even an intense emotion. Most changelings shifted their appearance fast enough to make a normal human think their eyes were playing tricks on them. But every changeling I'd known shifted the same way—their flesh actually flowed into the new form. None of them winked a new shape into existence and then out again like I'd just seen Katie Kennan do. If that really was Katie Kennan.

Well, even if she wasn't the real thing, she was the closest I had to the person I'd been hired to find. I slipped off my squeaky shoes, shoved them in the pockets of my raincoat, and followed her to the restroom.

Like public restrooms in any older shopping area, the Ladies Room in this mall was smaller and smellier than any bathroom I'd voluntarily be in if it wasn't absolutely necessary. It also had the obligatory line of women waiting for an open stall. I pretended to stand in line and waited for Katie.

And it was Katie, not the elf woman, who came out of the stall closest to the back wall. I half-expected her to find a secret door in the wall and walk through it given the way my luck had been running lately, but she didn't. Instead she walked over to the row of sinks and washed her hands, just like everyone else. Only when she looked up at herself in the mirror, did she do something unexpected.

She took one look at her reflection and froze, her hand halfway toward the paper towel holder.

I watched as her mouth dropped open in surprise. That look of surprise stayed on her face right up until the moment she saw my reflection in the mirror, then it turned to one of anger.

She made a beeline for the exit, but I blocked her path.

"Katie Kennan?" I said. "I've been looking for you."

She shook her head. "I'm not who you think I am."

"You look like it to me."

She tried to get past me. I forgot all about the fact that if whoever I've been hired to find doesn't want to be found, I usually let it go at that. I had too many questions for this woman, whoever she was, and the number one question was what in the world she was doing with my partner.

I reached out and grabbed her by the arm.

She sighed. "Okay," she said. "You got me."

Her whole body seemed to shrink right in front of my eyes. By the time she was done, she was no bigger than Seamus Flannery. Good thing her clothes shrank with her. Doubly good thing I had the presence of mind to hang onto her arm.

"You know the score," she said. "You get three wishes."

I blinked. "You're really a leprechaun?"

She rolled her eyes. "Your partner led me to believe you're smarter than that."

My partner. Oh, boy. I might have made a promise to Seamus Flannery, but it looked like Katie Kennan wasn't going to let me keep it. She'd already involved Diz in this... this, whatever it was.

"Let's go," I said.

I held onto Katie and marched her out into the corridor where she'd left my partner. Diz did a double-take when he saw us. I don't think I've ever seen him do that before.

"Meet Katie Kennan," I said to my partner. "I was hired by her business partner this morning to find her."

"That's nice," Diz said. "What's that got to do with me?"

I looked at Katie. "Show him," I said.

She glared at me. "It won't work if you're watching me."

"Fine. But I'm not letting go."

I turned my head. The stores that lined the corridor all had plate glass storefronts. I managed to catch a glimpse of Katie's reflection as she went from diminutive leprechaun to full-sized elf. When I turned back around, she stayed full-sized, but now she wore Katie Kennan's face.

"I'll be damned," Diz said. "That's some glamour. I never felt it. How'd you do that?"

I remembered the part of my vision in which Seamus Flannery was trying to break free of a chain. If he was chained up somewhere, he couldn't have met with me.

"That was you in my office this morning, right?" I asked.

She nodded.

"How'd you do that?"

She didn't smile, but her eyes glittered with mischief. "I'll tell you everything you want to know, if you wish it."

I thought about that. I'd never been in a position to have three wishes to play with. I knew all the old stories about being careful what you wished for, that you just might get it, but I'd become a detective because I wanted to find answers. I'm not too proud to admit that this whole investigation had me confused enough I might have to hand in my private detective's super-secret handbook.

Not that anyone's actually given me a super-secret handbook.

"Okay," I said slowly, trying to frame my words right. "My first wish is to know why you hired me to find... well, you. In other words, my wish is to know what's going on here."

Katie smiled at me. "It's quite the tale. Can I suggest that we find a quiet place to talk?"

Diz found us an empty table in a small courtyard that connected Rainbow Condoms' building to the one next door. Well, found is a slight exaggeration. Two teenage boys had been sitting at the table nursing sodas, their hamburgers long gone. Diz had glared at them, and when the glare didn't work, he upped the wattage into a full glower.

The boys had fled, and we sat down. I kept a firm hold on Katie's arm even though she assured me it wasn't necessary. I kinda didn't believe her.

"I'm not the original Katie Kennan," she said. "Seamus granted me the gift of mimicry as my first wish. I become whoever a person expects to see."

"I thought leprechauns only granted wishes when they're captured," Diz said.

"You knew that part of the legend was true?" I asked him.

He shrugged. "Legends have to come from somewhere."

I stared at Katie. "You lied to me."

She smiled. The mischief was back in her eyes. "You hadn't captured me then. And I didn't lie. I only implied there was no truth to the legend."

I sighed. "Potato, potahto. Go on with the story."

She put her elbows on the table. I kept a firm grip on her arm.

"I was but a poor daughter of an even poorer shoe maker," she said. "Not a rich, famous cobbler like Seamus. There's a reason we're solitary creatures, we leprechauns. If anyone captures us, we use our magic granting wishes, but using those magics diminishes what we work so hard to accumulate."

"Your gold," I said.

She nodded. "My father was never very good at hiding, so he was always poor. Seamus was very good at it, but he'd become bold over the years, loving his Katie as he did. She used him, but he didn't see it. Couldn't see it, poor wee lad. When she finally left him, I told him I'd be his Katie for him, and he, generous soul that he was, granted me the ability to become whatever anyone expected." She looked at me. "Or whatever I needed to be. This morning, I needed to be Seamus for you." She turned to Diz. "For you, I became your sister."

Diz had a sister? I didn't know whether to be surprised or relieved. Diz never talked about his family.

"You haven't explained it all, not yet," I said. "Why hire me to find the person you were pretending to be all along?"

Her eyes twinkled. "Well, you see, the second thing Seamus granted me was wealth, knowing that I come from such a poor family. But he played a trick on me. We've been known to do that from time to time. Play tricks with our wishes."

I caught the warning. I still had two wishes left, but now I wasn't sure I wanted to use them.

"These were wishes he granted you?" Diz asked.

"Not precisely."

I wondered how not precisely. Apparently the old legends only scratched the surface of the leprechaun playbook.

"He hid my wealth from me," Katie said. "Combined it with his in that pot he keeps hidden. I played along for a while, but after a few decades, I grew tired of the game. Seamus must have realized that I would, and what the third thing would be that I'd want from him."

"The location of the gold," Diz said.

"Yes," she said. "So Seamus did something I never expected."

I remembered my vision—Seamus pounding away at a chain. He wasn't trying to break it, but trying to make sure the chain was solid so he couldn't change his mind and go back to this greedy creature he'd shackled himself to.

"He locked himself away," I said. "Hid himself away from you."

Katie smiled. It wasn't pleasant. "Oh, but you are clever. I knew I hired the right person. Anyone who could outfox Eros, I thought to myself, would be the perfect person to find Seamus and his gold."

"But you didn't hire me to find Seamus and his gold," I said.

"Of course not, dearie. Would you have taken the case if I had? I think not. But you would take the case of a heartbroken little man searching for the love of his life, so I had to become Seamus and hope that that little ability of yours would lead me to him."

My "little ability."

She'd played me, just like she'd played Seamus. Was I that transparent? And if someone like Katie Kennan, or whatever her true name was, could read me, did that mean Diz knew about my fantasies? I felt my cheeks heat up.

"You were wrong," I said. "I don't know where Seamus or his gold are. I can't help you."

She looked at me for a long moment, no doubt trying to decide whether I was playing her now.

I looked her in the eye and told myself that what I'd said was the truth. I didn't know where Seamus and his gold were. I just had a hunch. Where else in Moretown Bay could a person find a permanent rainbow? Even after Rainbow Condoms had gone out of business, the sign with their logo—complete with stylized rainbow—remained on their storefront. There had to be a reason for that. I wouldn't be surprised if Seamus had a private little storage room two or three levels down, complete with an over-flowing pot of gold.

Eventually, Katie sighed. "You did catch me out at my own game, it seems. No matter. I'll try again. I have Seamus's company, and I've managed to keep whatever profits I've made above what he expected when he left. I'll do fine."

No wonder she had become Kate the Terrible. Cobblerstones hadn't suffered from a run of bad luck but rather from the cost-cutting, money-grubbing measures of its one remaining owner. I rather doubted she'd reap all that much money for her own pot of gold before she ran Flannery's entire company into the ground.

"I still have two wishes left?" I asked her.

"Dee." Diz's voice had more than just a hint of a warning. "Leprechauns are fairies. Remember that."

I knew what Diz was trying to tell me. It was the first rule I'd learned as a cop when I transferred to the Bureau of Magical Enforcement: Don't Make Bargains With Fairies. Fairy bargains always turned out badly for the non-fey involved.

But I wasn't going to make a bargain. I was going to use my two remaining wishes.

"My second wish," I said, looking right in Katie's eyes, "is that Seamus forget all about you."

Her green eyes gleamed. I knew what she was thinking. If Seamus forgot about her, he'd forget that he needed to hide himself and his gold from her. He'd come out of hiding on his own, and she'd have a second chance to trick him all over again.

"Done," she said. "And your third wish?" She leaned toward me. "I can give you what your heart desires." Her voice was pitched low, but Diz was an elf. He'd have no problem hearing her. "You just have to ask."

I didn't look at my partner. I didn't want Diz's attentions, not if I had to rely on magic to get them. If my fantasies were going to come true someday, I wanted it to happen naturally.

No, I had something else in mind. I thought about the little man I hadn't really met, the little man who only wanted to recreate a once-in-a-lifetime love. I looked at the fey creature I gripped by the arm. She really was no different than a lot of people I knew. She wanted to be rich, and she didn't care how she got there. I couldn't do anything about the people they hurt. I could do something about her.

"My third wish," I told this false Katie Kennan, "is that you forget all about Seamus and his gold."

The look of shocked surprise on her face as she realized she had no choice but to grant my wish was the best thing that had happened to me all day.

THAT NIGHT, Diz and I sat in the front office eating Chinese takeout. My cat was curled up on the loveseat next to Diz. I sat at my desk in my battered executive chair staring at my food.

"Well, at least she paid us in cash," I said.

I usually felt good at the end of a case. Even when a case ended with me negotiating a tense truce between warring family members, at least I felt like I'd accomplished something. This time all I felt was used up and more than a little sad.

My cat was purring up a storm. Of course, she was curled up next to Diz. I'd purr if I was curled up next to Diz, too. I could have been in my cat's place if I'd made a different wish, but I didn't think I could have lived with myself if I had.

I poked at the food with my chopsticks. I wasn't really hungry.

Diz hopped off the loveseat without disturbing the cat. Even though he's got a bodybuilder's physique, he's as graceful and light on his feet as every other elf I've known, and that's pretty darn cool.

"I think you need a massage," he said.

94

We'd celebrated the end of Eros's case with a two-for-one massage from the masseuse across the street. Back when I'd suggested the idea, I'd hoped we'd end up on adjoining tables, but the two-for-one deal only meant the price. We'd been ushered into separate rooms, which is why I'd only gotten a brief glimpse of my partner's towel-covered derriere.

"Great idea," I said, trying to work up a smile. "But she's closed for the night."

Diz walked around behind me. "That's not what I meant," he said.

He brushed my frizzy hair away from my shoulders. I tried to suppress a shiver.

Diz was going to give me a backrub? Oh, my. If he was any good at all, I'd be in serious trouble here. A truly great backrub was better than sex. Or so I've heard.

His fingers found the exact spot where my muscles were the tightest. I tried not to groan as he worked those muscles loose.

"You did good work today," he said. "She used us both, but we got lucky. We stopped her before she went too far."

Lucky? My new tennies had sprung a serious leak on the way home. I only hoped that once Seamus was back in charge of production, Cobblerstones would still be in business. I really did like those shoes.

"There's one thing I still don't understand," I said.

"What's that?"

"Why did she appear to you as your sister?"

I felt him shrug. "My sister's the only member of my

family I can stand," Diz said. "Most of them didn't agree with me working as a cop. Ella's the only one who supported me. Plus, she's the only one who ever leaves the island. Last time I heard from her, she said she was going to stop by and see me soon."

Before today, all I knew about Diz's family was that they were part of a clan of wood elves who lived on Marlette Island on the west side of the Bay. Most of the island was heavily timbered, and the elves worked hard to keep it that way.

"So that's who you expected to see when our little mimic showed up."

"You got it."

"Ella, huh?" I bet I knew who she was named after.

Diz sighed. "My mother was consistent, I'll give her that."

"But why did she go to such great lengths to spend time with you in the first place?" I asked. "I don't understand that at all."

His fingers stopped moving on my back. "She needed to keep us apart. Keep me busy and hope that your visions told you where Seamus hid himself."

"Because I'm the gullible one." I didn't feel very good about that. I'd always thought I had a better bullshit meter than that.

"No. Because it cost her more magical energy to become someone you've never seen before. I expected to see my sister. You had no reason to expect Seamus Flannery."

I got it then. Like all elves, Diz could sense magic. He

told me once it felt like a tingle on his skin whenever he ran across a current of magical energy nearby. He would know how much was normal for a leprechaun—or for an elf, for that matter. When little Katie mimicked a much taller someone Diz expected to see, like his sister, the tingle would have felt elf normal, for lack of a better term, to Diz. But if he'd been around when little Katie was working hard to pull off her illusion of little Seamus, the false Seamus would have pinged off the scale for Diz.

"I guess that means we work better as a team," I said.

Diz snorted. "You just now figured that out?"

I started to say something else, but my smart retort dissolved into a happy sigh as Diz found just the perfect spot at the base of my neck and began his massage all over again. I let my head fall forward, grateful that my hair hid what was no doubt a silly, sated expression on my face.

"I think you've been hanging around your cat too long," Diz said after a few minutes.

"Mmfpht?" I breathed out and tried again. "Why's that?"

Diz leaned toward me, and when he spoke again, his voice came from right behind my left ear. "You're purring."

What do you know. He was right.

I was.

Guess I'm pretty darn lucky after all.

MY COUSIN, THE RABBIT

I was balancing my morning coffee and a bag of donuts in one hand and fumbling with the key to my office with the other when my cell phone rang.

I'm not a morning person. I'm also not the world's greatest cook. Even though I live in the apartment upstairs from my office, I go out most mornings for coffee and something my mother would not approve of as breakfast food. So when I recognized the ring tone I'd assigned to my mother—a snazzy little number that sounded like the music from Psycho right about the time Anthony Perkins goes gonzo on Janet Leigh with a knife in the shower—my first reaction was to drop the bag of donuts like a hot potato.

What? Donuts? Not me, mom. I'm going upstairs to fix myself sprouts and granola right this minute.

Not that I had sprouts and granola in my apartment. I barely had enough food for my cat.

The bag split open when it hit the sidewalk, spilling

all that sugary goodness on the wet concrete. So much for breakfast. At least I still had my coffee.

I managed to get the office door unlocked and my cell phone out of my pocket before the call rang over to voicemail.

"Your cousin's missing," my mother said before I could even croak out a hello.

No wonder she was calling me at this ungodly hour. Along with my partner, I run D & D Investigations, and as the sign on our front window says, Missing Persons Are Our Specialty. Since my mother was calling me and not the police, I knew which cousin had to be missing.

Unlike a lot of people, I only have two cousins. My cousin Stacy lives with her perfect husband and two perfect children in a perfect little house in an exclusive— and very expensive—neighborhood on the south end of Marlette Island. I live across the Bay in a dinky one-bedroom apartment on the second floor of my office building, which happens to be located in a not-very-exclusive neighborhood on the mainland side of More-town Bay. If perfect Stacy had gone missing, my mother wouldn't be calling me. She'd have called out the National Guard.

That left only one cousin.

"Harold?" I asked.

"Harold," my mother said. "Gloria's a mess."

Gloria is my aunt, my mom's older sister. Harold is Aunt Gloria's son. He's ten years older than I am, single like me, but unlike me, he still lives with his mother.

I sighed and settled into my semi-battered executive

chair behind my battered wooden desk. D & D Investigations manages to keep its doors open—barely—but our furnishings are strictly second-hand, garage sale rejects. Not that I'm complaining. My chair may have seen better days, but it's darn comfortable.

I peeled the plastic lid off my coffee and inhaled the aroma, trying not to think about the donuts melting into a gooey mess on the sidewalk thanks to this morning's misty rain. Our office building used to house a bakery, and it still smells sugary sweet when it's damp, like this morning. Well, like nearly every morning in Moretown Bay. There's a reason my hair frizzes more than curls. Right now the ghostly smell of Croissants Past was making my stomach grumble, and coffee alone wasn't going to cut it.

Not if my day was going to be spent chasing my missing cousin.

"Want to tell me what happened?" I asked my mother.

"He didn't come home from work last night, so Gloria called Mr. Fistler."

Of Fistler's Fine Furnishings, where I'd bought my semi-battered executive chair. The furnishings Frederick Fistler sold weren't fine in the sense of rare or unique, but more in the sense of they'll do fine in a pinch. Old man Fistler had given Harold a job when no one else would, so that made him more than okay in my book.

"Mr. Fistler told Gloria that Harold left at noon yesterday," my mother said. "Harold said he had some errands to run and he'd be back late, only he never came back. Gloria spent the night calling all Harold's friends, only none of them had seen him all day and no one had any idea what kind of errands he was running."

I pinched the bridge of my nose. My mother and my Aunt Gloria tried to maintain the impression that Harold was just fine, that he had friends and a regular social life and ran errands like everyone else. I knew better. If Harold had more friends than I could count on the fingers of one hand, I was an elf.

I'm not an elf, by the way. The elf half of D & D Investigations is my partner, Diz, and a gorgeous elf at that, if in a grouchy, The Rock kind of way. I'm a regular old mortal like my mom and my Aunt Gloria and poor missing Harold. Well, maybe not exactly like the rest of my family.

"Can't you do that thing?" my mother asked.

That's why she was really calling me. "That thing," as my mother calls it, is the bit of magic sight that sometimes lets me catch a glimpse of things that are about to happen. My mother doesn't have any great confidence in my abilities as a hit-the-streets, work-the-clues kind of detective. She does, however, think I have a crystal ball inside my skull that lets me see the future. She believes in my ability to predict what's going to happen as much as she believes in the spiritual advice she gets from her neighbor who reads tarot cards for all the women in Merlin Heights, the subdivision where my mother and father have lived for the last forty years.

No matter how many times I've told my mother that

my precog ability doesn't work that way, she still insists on telling people I'm her little fortune teller.

"I'll make some calls," I said just as Diz opened the front door.

He raised a cinnamon-hued eyebrow at me. I mouthed *my mother* and pointed at my cell phone. He placed a white paper bag on my desk and tiptoed into the back office.

Not that Diz has to tiptoe, precisely. For a guy with a bodybuilder's physique, he's light on his feet like all elves I've ever met. I'd threaten to make him wear a bell around his neck like the one my cat has on her collar, but have I mentioned that Diz is one strong elf? I'm not sure why he puts up with me, but the last thing I want to do is rock the boat. One of the perks of running my own detective agency, besides not having to wear a uniform like I did when I first started working as a cop, is that Diz is my partner.

"You don't think... " My mother left the rest of the thought unspoken, but I knew what she meant. While Harold didn't have many friends, he did have one enemy.

"I'll check that out, too," I said. "Tell Aunt Gloria she should try not to worry."

My mother let out a humorous laugh. "What's to worry about, right? It's probably just the time of year. Harold never did like Easter."

I suppose if I'd been turned into a six-foot tall white rabbit when I was fifteen years old, I might not like Easter too much either.

I WAS TOO young at the time to know exactly what happened to Harold, but I've heard the story about how my poor cousin rubbed the wrong adolescent wizard the wrong way and ended up eating a ton of carrots for a week.

It all started over a girl.

To hear my Aunt Gloria tell it, Harold had planned for weeks to ask a pretty little wood nymph to the spring dance. Aunt Gloria lives four blocks away from my mother and father, so Harold and I went to the same high school a decade apart. The Merlin Heights High School accepted all the kids in the neighborhood—human, elf, troll, goblin, nymph—the place was an equal opportunity torture chamber, or at least it was when I went there. I can't imagine school was any better for my cousin when he walked the halls of old Merlin High a decade earlier.

Magic users got bored out of their minds same as us vanilla mortals, only where mortals were sent to the principal's office for harmless little pranks like passing notes in class, magic users found themselves in the principal's office for setting those notes on fire. Springtime pranks were the worst because by then, the whole student body—magic users and mortals alike—were ready to cut loose on spring break.

The dance was the last big shindig before a week's reprieve from listening to Mr. Elliot drone on about textile production in South America. I'm not sure what textile production in South America had to do with Civics, which was the official title of Mr. Elliot's spring semester class, but Mr. Elliot taught the same thing year after year, leaving decades of sophomores with little more to do in his class but pass notes and think about who's going with who to the dance.

Going with whom. I think I daydreamed my way through English, too.

I frankly can't imagine Harold ever asking anyone to a dance. The Harold I've always known is so shy he spends most of the time looking at his shoes while people are trying to talk to him. Now, if Harold was as handsome as George Clooney, no problem. Unfortunately for Harold, no such luck. Back in high school, he looked more like the skinny kid with the big ears everyone always picked on in road trip movies. Even now, Harold's not exactly a big man. Mr. Fistler had Harold working in the back, keeping track of invoices and inventory, for a reason. Even Mr. Fistler knew Harold wasn't the kind of guy who could chat up the customers.

So I don't think Harold intended to ask the wood nymph to the dance. He just daydreamed about it.

That made Harold the mortal enemy of one Gil Blackthorne.

Gil had a crush on the wood nymph, too, and Gil was a budding wizard. Although I doubted it took much magical ability to see that Harold was crushing on the same girl.

Conventional wisdom says that magical ability kicks in around puberty for mortals born with latent magical gifts. I'm not sure if that's true for anyone else, but my precog visions kicked in around that time, which made my teenage years all sorts of fun. I'm the only one I know of in my family with any magical talent, so I had no one to really talk to about what was happening to me.

I don't know if Gil Blackthorne had any wizards in his family he could talk to, or if he decided all on his own that being a wizard was just one more step in his plan for total high school domination. But like any wannabe king, Gil had already picked out his queen—the wood nymph —and heaven help anyone he felt stood in his way.

Aunt Gloria makes the inevitable confrontation between Harold the Determined and Gil the Wizard sound like the gunfight at the O.K. Corral. I have a feeling it was more like Gil the Bully pinning Harold the Meek against the lockers in an attempt to intimidate a potential rival who wouldn't say boo to a ghost. I'm not sure if Harold actually tried to stand up for himself or if Gil was just feeling the rush of a new power he didn't know how to control, but when the confrontation ended, my cousin was a six-foot tall white rabbit.

Gil got suspended and was told he couldn't come back until he reversed the spell. Only Gil never bothered to learn a reversal spell. It took the better part of a week for Gil to figure out how to turn my cousin human again.

Harold's never quite gotten over the experience. I can't say that I blame him.

When I got off the phone with my mother, I opened the white paper bag Diz had left on my desk. At the bottom of the bag was a perfect cherry turnover.

"I think I'm in love," I muttered as I lifted the pastry out of the bag.

"You are, are you?"

I blinked. Diz was leaning on the door jamb, blocking the doorway between the front office where we interview clients and the back office where we kept our computer equipment and mounds of unfiled paperwork hidden from potential clients.

I so needed to get my partner a bell.

I shoved the turnover in my mouth so I wouldn't have to think of something to say.

Okay, I admit it. I've got something of a crush of my own on my partner. Or I would have, if I was still in high school. I'm not sure someone who's pushing thirty is allowed to have a crush, but whatever this feeling is, it only got stronger after I discovered that Diz, my perpetually grumpy partner, gives the world's best backrubs. And now he brings me pastry? I should be excused from temporarily forgetting I shouldn't blurt out something, even under my breath, that my pointy-eared partner would have no trouble hearing.

I decided to pretend the whole thing never happened.

"My mother just hired us," I said when I got done with my mouthful of flakey cherry goodness.

"Hired us? As in, she's paying us?"

"Well, maybe hired is the wrong word. My cousin's missing. She asked me to help find him."

I relayed what my mother had told me, then I filled Diz in on what little I knew about Harold's teenage altercation with Gil Blackthorne, a wizard with a seriously villainous-sounding name.

"You think he's behind your cousin's disappearance?" Diz asked.

I sighed. Elves have an incredibly long life span. For an elf, twenty-five years is a blink of the eye. For mere mortals like Harold, high school was another lifetime ago.

"It would be a long shot," I said. "If anything, the side effects of what Blackthorne did are what's caused Harold to go AWOL. No matter what my Aunt Gloria thinks, Harold's not the kind of guy who makes a lot of friends. He kind of comes unhinged this time of year, what with all the Easter Bunny stuff on television and in the stores." Heck, even the masseuse across the street had a cartoon Easter Bunny painted on her front window. Hop right in for a bunny-rific backrub! said the text next to the rabbit.

"How do we know Fistler's telling the truth?" Diz asked. "He could have something to do with Harold's disappearance."

"Fistler sold me this chair," I said.

Diz glowered at my semi-battered executive chair. He'd tried sitting in it once, but he said it wasn't comfortable. This from an elf who scales the outside of buildings for fun.

"Okay, so we start with Fistler," I said, capitulating to the glower. "And if he doesn't pan out—"

"We'll find this Blackthorne guy."

We had a plan. Now I just had to hope that when we

found Harold, I wouldn't be taking a six-foot tall white rabbit home to my aunt.

FISTLER'S Fine Furnishings was in an aging shopping center a couple of miles from Merlin Heights. In addition to Fistler's furniture warehouse, the shopping center was home to a Sears store, a second-run movie theater, a used bookstore, and a curio and collectibles shop that had a sign in the window saying they specialized in antique magical accoutrements.

Diz glowered at the sign. "Tourist trap," he said.

I could understand the tourist trap remark if the store was one of shops in the touristy waterfront area of Moretown Bay. The Moretown Bay city council had spent a ton of money turning empty warehouses into quirky little stores and delis and specialty shops, liberally salted with pubs and street musicians and tame magical acts meant to entertain, not frighten, non-magical folk and encourage them to spend all the money they could afford and then some. This old shopping center was nowhere near a tourist area. It couldn't even rightly be called an outdoor mall. Except for one small strip of stores that included the bookstore and curio shop, all the buildings were free-standing with a mostly empty parking area in the middle. The place even had an old-fashioned coffee shop that fronted the street. Most of the cars in the lot were parked close to the coffee shop.

"What exactly are 'antique magical accoutrements'?" I asked.

"Cracked crystal balls, most likely."

"But not magical," I said.

"Not a chance."

I believed him. Diz, like most elves, can sense magic. He described it to me once as feeling a tingle on his skin whenever he ran across a nearby current of magical energy. He would have sensed if any of the items in the curio shop held the kind of magical current, even antique magical current, that would have made them the genuine articles.

I parked in front of the used bookstore. Diz shot me a look out of the corner of his eye. He knew me well.

See, I liked to read. Okay, I liked to read a lot. I couldn't afford cable TV, and a girl could only spend so many nights watching her cat groom before it got old. I thought I knew where all the used bookstores in More-town Bay were located, but I'd never heard of Browsers Books before. The bookstore hadn't been here the last time I'd been to this shopping center when I'd bought my chair. The lure to go exploring among unfamiliar racks of well-loved paperbacks was almost irresistible.

"Your cousin, the rabbit, remember?" Diz said.

I sighed. "Okay. We go talk to Mr. Fistler first, then I'll do a quick in and out through the bookstore. No more than five minutes."

"Dee..."

"Ten tops. I promise."

"Ten," Diz said. "Then I'm going to find this Black-thorne guy by myself."

He'd do it too. Patience is not an elfen trait that Diz possesses. Nor serenity. Nor calm appreciation of the natural world. Diz would rather interrogate a suspect than watch a tree grow. It's no wonder Diz left his clan's enclave on the wooded northern end of Marlette Island to become a cop.

That's where we first partnered up, in the Moretown Bay Police Department. We both worked for the Bureau of Magical Enforcement. Diz got stuck with me because no one else wanted to work with a vanilla mortal, and a woman at that, whose magical abilities barely qualified her to work for the BME, and I got stuck with Diz because no one else wanted to work with his grumpy elf self. I've never been quite sure why Diz stuck with me after we both left the force, but I'm glad he did. I'm also glad he's not quite as grumpy these days as he was back when we were both cops. Maybe he didn't like the uniforms either.

Fistler's Fine Furnishings was in a big free-standing building at the back of the shopping center next to the used bookstore. The building was painted a dull brick red with trim that might have been white at one time but had faded to grey in the constant, salty humidity of Moretown Bay. The lettering on the sign over the door was Old English and more than a little difficult to read, and the plate glass windows at the front of the store were foggy with age. Still, from the outside I could see that the place was crammed to the gills with used furniture, just like it had been the last time I was here.

We walked through the double doors at the entrance, and I caught the almost imperceptible pause in Diz's stride.

I gave him a questioning look. In response, he curled his right hand into a loose fist.

It was an old signal that we used to use when we were on the force. It meant someone in the store was using magic, and that it was strong enough that Diz was concerned. The loose fist meant he thought it was something we could handle. A tight fist would have meant "run like hell and call for backup."

All sorts of magical folk use magical energy like mortals use the air to breathe. They can't help it, it's just part of who they are. Changelings, for instance, appear to most people as anything except what they truly are, which I understand isn't easy for mortals to look at. I've never seen a changeling "out of character," so to speak, and Diz told me once I should be thankful for that.

Diz wouldn't react with a curled fist to that kind of magic use. No, the curled fist meant Diz was sensing manipulated magic, like something a conjurer would do.

Or a wizard.

Only what was a wizard doing conjuring magic in Fistler's Fine Furnishings?

It was hard for me to see whether anyone was browsing between the rows of bookcases and armoires and entertainment centers that crowded the front of the store. I'm not the tallest person in the world. In fact, the top of my head barely makes it to Diz's shoulder.

Diz didn't have that problem. Overhead was a spider web of pipes and ductwork all painted the same dull brick red as the ceiling and the outside of the building. One minute Diz was standing next to me, and the next he'd leapt from the top level of a set of bunk beds to a pipe a good ten feet over his head. I watched him swing himself up on the pipe like a gymnast, and then he started walking on top of the pipe like he'd done it all his life.

He'd probably tell me it was an elf thing. I made a mental note to add it to my ever-growing list of elf things.

Since I was stuck on the ground, I decided the best thing to do was go find my cousin's boss.

Frederick Fistler was in his sixties. He was a sturdy man who looked like he might have been an athlete in his younger years. He's mortal, from what I could tell, anyway, and he had a full head of hair that was mostly pepper with a little steel-grey salt mixed in here and there. His fingers were thick-knuckled, his eyebrows bushy, and he had a thin mustache that just about covered a scar that ran along his upper lip.

Fistler had set aside a small space at the back of his store where he did whatever repairs were necessary on the secondhand furniture he sold. When I found him, he was wearing a leather apron with big pockets that held all sorts of well-worn tools of his trade.

"Dee!" he called out to me in a voice that didn't

sound like it belonged to a sixty-year-old. "Have you found him?"

I shook my head. "I'm just getting started. Mother only called me this morning."

He looked as upset as my mother had sounded. "Harold's a good boy, but he lets this time of year get to him."

I didn't know if Mr. Fistler knew why, so I decided not to mention the rabbit thing. "You told Aunt Gloria that Harold left yesterday to run errands?"

Fistler nodded. "That's what he told me. I thought it was strange. Harold rarely leaves for lunch—he eats back at his desk—and I can't remember the last time he asked to leave early. If anything, I have to kick him out at night so I can go home."

"Did he seem upset?"

"I don't think so, but I didn't actually see him leave. I was in the back. He just called me on the intercom." Fistler pointed at the telephone, so I guessed the phones had speakers.

"So you don't know if any customers were in the store."

Fistler made a gesture that was half-shrug, half *I'm only one man, what can I do?* "I don't have any security cameras in the front," he said. "Who would steal a bookcase or a bed? I only have a camera over the register."

Over the register. That wouldn't do me any good. Harold didn't work the register.

Except Fistler said he'd been in the back.

"When you work back here, do you go up front and

run the register? Or does Harold take over if you're busy?"

"If I have my hands full, Harold knows how to run the register. I try not to do that to him often. He's not good with people."

That was putting it mildly.

"What about yesterday?" I asked. "Did he run the register for you yesterday?"

I could see Fistler thinking about it. He shook his head. "I only had a few sales yesterday. I rang them all up myself."

So much for that idea.

Or maybe not. Paying for a purchase wasn't the only reason customers came up to come to the counter.

"Do you still have yesterday's security footage?" I asked.

"Yes, I think so. It's on the computer."

"Mind if I look?"

Fistler took me in the business office where we sat at what had to be Harold's desk. A gold-framed picture of Stacy and her perfect husband and her two perfect children was off to one side of the computer monitor, and a smiling picture of my Aunt Gloria was in a small silver frame on the other side. An old-fashioned desk blotter, the kind with a monthly paper calendar in the center, took up most of the desk space in front of the monitor. Easter Sunday was X'd out so many times that the x's had ripped through the paper.

Diz glided into the office without a sound. He cleared his throat to let Fistler know he was there. I wondered if

I'd muttered about the bell when I thought I was just grumbling to myself.

"My partner," I told Fistler. "Okay with you if he watches, too? His eyes are better than mine."

Fistler blinked at Diz, who for once was actually trying to look non-threatening. "Better than mine, too," Fistler said, and he moved out of the way as yesterday's video started to play.

Fistler had the video playing at triple speed so it wouldn't take us ten hours to watch. Most of the time, the camera showed only an empty counter and a closed register. The date and time was displayed in the lower right hand corner. It was more interesting to watch the numbers speed by on the digital display than concentrate on the empty register. Thank you, Mr. Elliot, for teaching me the fine art of distracting myself from a boring presentation. The lesson I should have taken from your class, instead of memorizing outdated facts about South American textiles, was that not all things that appear boring at first blush are useless.

The time stamp on the recording read 1:23 p.m. when someone actually moved into the frame. I could tell from the top of his head that the man at the register was Harold. His hair had always been a little thin on top, and now that he'd hit his forties, it was easy to see the shine of his scalp through what was left of his hair.

I hit the program control that slowed the security footage to real time speed. A man and a woman stood on the customer side of the counter.

"Wood nymph," Diz said.

The security camera footage was in black and white, and the man had on a wide-brimmed hat. It was impossible to get a good look at his face above the nose, but I could see he had a dark little goatee. The woman was all patterned skin and dark, pixie-cut hair with a fine-featured face.

I thought back to the story of why Harold had been turned into a rabbit in the first place. A wood nymph had been involved back then, too.

Diz met my gaze, and I knew what he was thinking. It couldn't be the same wood nymph, could it? More-town Bay wasn't a huge city, but it wasn't a backwoods burg, either. Wood nymphs were pretty common in an area as heavily forested as the land to the east of the city. Then again, Fistler's Fine Furniture was only a couple of miles away from where Harold had grown up as a boy, and wood nymphs didn't age as fast as mortals.

"Do you know who this is?" I asked Fistler.

"I do," said a new voice.

I turned around to see another wood nymph come into the office from the back of the store where Fistler did his repairs.

"Keesa," Fistler said. "My assistant."

Assistant?

He held up his large-knuckled hands. "Arthritis," he said. "My hands can't work the wood the way they used to, so Keesa helps me out. She's got a way with the wood, brings out the luster in even the oldest pieces I have in the shop."

I bet she did.

I glanced at Diz to see if that was the magical energy he'd felt in the store. He shook his head slightly to let me know it wasn't. Keesa might be using her natural talents to enhance all of Fistler's wooden furniture, but something else was going on here that had more to do with conjuring than enhancement.

"Who are the people on the monitor?" I asked Keesa.

"My sister." She pointed at the monitor, and for a split second, the picture winked out. Keesa dropped her hand, and the picture came back.

"Did she grow up around here?" I asked.

"We both did," Keesa said. "Although she lived among more people than I did."

It couldn't be.

"Who's the guy?" Diz asked.

Keesa scrunched up her nose. I didn't know a lot of wood nymph customs, but I was pretty sure that meant the same thing, human or nymph.

"Her employer," Keesa said. "He's a stage magician. He needed a new cabinet last week for his act. My sister knew I worked here and that the wood would be happy to leave me to go with her."

A stage magician. "What's his name?" I asked.

"I don't know his real name. He goes by the title The Great Blackthorne."

Bingo. It was all starting to fall into place.

"Did Harold see this man when they came in last week?" I asked.

The nymph shook her head.

"Do you know where he performs?"

The wood nymph shook her head again. It didn't matter. With a name like The Great Blackthorne, I could google the guy and figure out where he'd be.

Speaking of googling...

I brought up the Internet browser on Harold's computer and looked through the history. It was a good idea, but if my cousin had looked up any information on Blackthorne, he'd erased that search from his computer's history.

Of course, he wouldn't need a search if he had simply followed the guy. That was assuming Harold had followed Blackthorne, and the only way I could see that happening was if the nymph with Blackthorne was Harold's old high school crush.

"Did your sister go to high school here?" I asked the nymph.

"High school?" She looked confused. "I don't understand."

"What does high school have to do any of this?" Fistler asked.

If Harold hadn't told Fistler about his adventures as a rabbit, I wasn't about to bring that up now. "Probably nothing," I said.

I didn't feel comfortable digging into Blackthorne any further on Fistler's computer. If this was the same Blackthorne, and I had no doubt that it was, he'd been a vengeful little wannabe wizard in high school. I'd be willing to bet he was an older vengeful wizard now. I didn't want anything I did bouncing back on Fistler. I could dig further into Blackthorne on my cell.

I thanked Fistler and Keesa and walked toward the front of the store. Diz fell into step beside me.

"He's more than a stage magician," Diz said.

"The magical energy?"

"Yeah. It's residual energy from when Blackthorne was here, only it's got a different feel to it. Like he combined his powers with the energy coming from the wood nymphs."

Combined his energy with theirs, or maybe he was sucking them dry. Harold was my cousin, and this guy had humiliated Harold. I wasn't feel too kindly toward Blackthorne right about then, and giving him the benefit of the doubt was a little beyond me.

I felt even less kindly toward him when I stepped out of the store and right into the middle of a precog vision.

I'M NOT A SHY PERSON, but I don't like being up on stage, either. One of my recurring nightmares as a kid was about having to recite the Gettysburg Address in front of a huge crowd of people while I stood all alone on stage, illuminated by a brilliant spotlight, wearing only my underwear. Mother told me it was only an anxiety dream, but I was probably the only second grader who had the entire Gettysburg Address memorized forwards and backwards. I wasn't taking any chances.

The vision I got in the parking lot in front of Fistler's Fine Furnishings took me right back to that old nightmare.

I was on stage illuminated by a brilliant spotlight. I could see far enough into the audience to know the auditorium was packed with more people than the entire waterfront tourist traps during the height of the summer season. I heard the rustle and murmurs of the audience even over the rasp of my own harsh breathing. I smelled pine and lemon, and felt a hard surface beneath my back and the rapid pounding of my heart.

Someone said something off to the right of me, and the crowd applauded. The sound was deafening, then the sound suddenly stopped. I could have heard a pin drop.

Which made the sudden snick and *thunk!* of metal sliding through the cabinet in which I was held even more startling.

Oh, crap! I was in the middle of a magic act.

Worse than that, I was the guinea pig locked inside one of those wooden cabinets made to show only my head and feet to the audience while the magician stuck swords through the wood in an attempt to impale me.

I made myself calm down. This was part of a magic trick, right? Swords weren't really going to plunge through me just for the sake of entertainment.

Were they?

I knew without looking at the magician that he had to be Gil Blackthorne from Merlin Heights High—The Amazing Blackthorne, as he called himself these days. I sincerely hoped my precog vision had something to do with Harold, because this whole vision was seriously creeping me out.

I had very little control over what a vision showed me, but I tried my hardest to look around on the stage to see anything that might tell me where the real Blackthorne was performing. I couldn't get the me in the vision to move much, but eventually I caught sight of an unused can light in the rafters over my head. The name of the theater was stenciled on the side of the light fixture: The Moretown Bay Concert Hall.

I knew where Blackthorne would be. The vision could end anytime now. Really. I'd rather not have it show me—in vivid, surround-sound pain—what would happen if Blackthorne cut me with one of those swords. I'd never died inside a precog vision before, so I don't know what would happen to the real me if I did. I'd rather not to find out now, thank you very much.

For once, it seemed like my vision heard me. The scene started to fuzz away to grey around the edges, and I could hear someone calling my name. Diz?

Just as I started to swim back to reality, my vision showed me one last thing.

A cage sitting on a black stool in the wings of the stage.

And inside the cage?

A white rabbit.

WE DROVE to the Moretown Bay Concert Hall as fast as traffic allowed. I tried telling myself that the rabbit had been too small to be Harold, but I wasn't doing a great job of convincing myself. Blackthorne had had a couple of decades to perfect the spell. Instead of turning my cousin into a six-foot tall rabbit, he'd managed to turn short, skinny Harold into a normal-sized bunny.

In a cage.

I might wring Blackthorne's scrawny neck myself—if he didn't turn me into a bunny first.

"How do you want to play this?" Diz asked.

"Just like we used to," I said.

"We don't have the cuffs anymore."

True. Back when we were cops, we were equipped with enchanted handcuffs. Once the handcuffs were snapped around a wizard's wrists—or any magic user's wrists—the cuffs kept them from using their magical energies. Enchantments like that gave cops an edge over magic-using bad guys. We weren't cops anymore. Those advantages were long gone.

We did still have us, though. My visions gave us a heads up on what the bad guy intended to do, and Diz's strength and speed let him get a jump on the bad guy himself. We'd taken down a few powerful wizards back when we'd been on the force. We'd also been pretty lucky not to end up toast a few times.

I wasn't going to think about that. Thanks to my vision, I knew Blackthorne was going to hold the audience enthralled with the swords-through-a-wooden-cabinet trick. If that was the cabinet he'd purchased from Fistler's Fine Furnishings, I had my doubts he'd actually had the time to refurbish it into a true gag cabinet. Was he counting on using real magic to pull off the trick?

The concert hall was a few blocks away from the tourist-laden shops near the fresh fish markets on the wharf. We managed to find a spot to park not too far away. The ticket lobby was filled with oversized posters advertising The Amazing Blackthorne. I bought tickets while Diz stalked around the lobby trying to get a read on the magical energy inside as well as the best way for us to get backstage without being hassled by security.

Diz doesn't do the Vulcan neck pinch or any Jedi mind tricks, but he does one damn fine intimidation glower. It's probably his build combined with the glower and topped off by a mullet. Yes, my partner wears his hair in a mullet. It's his least attractive quality, but considering all the other simply amazing ones, I'm not about to complain. Besides, between the mullet and the glare and the overall sense of barely restrained rage, I'm sure most people—like the poor concert hall security guard—thought Diz was about to go ballistic any second. People aren't used to dealing with grumpy elves. Mortals, especially, tend to get out of their way.

We made it backstage without any problems. Following my number one rule of detecting—act as if you belong—we blended in as much as we could with all the black-clad stage hands. When we found a relatively deserted spot, Diz left the stage and climbed up to the catwalk suspended over the stage. From there, we figured he could leap down and knock Blackthorne out before the wizard had a chance to turn his magic on us. Or, more precisely, me.

The plan was going along smoothly until Blackthorne's assistant, the wood nymph I thought might be Harold's long-lost, wannabe high school girlfriend, conked me on the back of the head and knocked me out.

I woke up to my all-time worst nightmare come true.

I was on stage, flat on my back inside one of those cut-the-girl-in-half boxes with a spotlight shining on me, and about a zillion people in the audience.

I squelched the little *meep!* that tried to escape my throat. Not the time to freeze up. Diz was still out there. He wouldn't let Blackthorne cut me in two, right?

I turned my head, and there he was—The Amazing Blackthorne.

If I hadn't been trapped in a box, I might have actually laughed. Mr. Amazing didn't look all that amazing to me. In fact, he didn't look all that different than my cousin. Short, skinny, big ears, and the kind of slouched shoulders that came from walking around with low self-esteem. He wore black silk trousers, a white silk shirt in a style that used to be called a poet's shirt—big billowy sleeves, the better to conceal tricks up, my dear—and a short black cape with a shiny purple lining. He actually held a wand in one hand while he gestured at me in the box with the other.

Someone tickled the bottom of my feet, which was the first time I realized my feet were bare and sticking out of the bottom of the box. I wriggled my toes and the audience laughed.

Oh, great. We who are about to die appreciate the laughter.

Where was my partner?

Right about then, I saw Diz up on the catwalk over my head. He was crouching on the catwalk, and he looked like he was getting ready to jump. I tore my gaze away so that The Amazing Blackthorne or his foot-tickling wood nymph assistant wouldn't catch a clue that Diz was about to unleash a whole lot of angry elf on their heads.

Only Diz never got the chance.

Right about the time I decided to close my eyes to keep from looking where I shouldn't, I heard the most awful war cry bellow out from behind the curtains, and this skinny, short, big-eared, middle-aged man rushed out on stage and cold-cocked The Amazing Blackthorne while the wizard was just starting to turn to meet the racket head-on.

The fight was short and sweet. Harold came equipped for battle. Not only did he knock Blackthorne out, he pressed a cloth over Blackthorne's nose, and the wizard went limp.

My shy, traumatized cousin had just saved the day. Chloroform would knock any human magic user out, wizard or not.

Diz leapt from the catwalk, ready to deal with the wood nymph, but he needn't have bothered. Once Black-thorne was down for the count, the nymph seemed to shake herself, then she looked at Harold and smiled the most brilliant smile I've ever seen.

My hero of a cousin turned into a shy teenager all over again. One of these days Harold was really going to have to learn how to talk to girls.

Probably to buy himself a little time, Harold came over and let me out of the Cabinet of Doom.

"Hey, cousin," I said, rubbing the back of my head. I don't know what the nymph had hit me with, but I was going to have a major headache.

Harold started to look down at his feet, but I could almost see him give himself a little pep talk. He met my gaze instead. "Hey, Dee."

I nodded at the white rabbit in the cage in the wings. "I was afraid that was going to be you, and I'd have to convince Blackthorne to lift the spell."

Harold gave me one of those looks. It's amazing how much that made him look like my mother.

"Sometimes, a rabbit's just a rabbit," he said.

WE WRAPPED up the Blackthorne case quickly. It turned out that the wood nymph had started as Blackthorne's willing assistant—he paid her pretty well—until he figured out a spell to hold her magic hostage. He threatened that he'd never give the nymph her magic back unless she did exactly what he said, including attack me, for which she apologized profusely. Once Harold knocked out Blackthorne with the chloroform, the spell was broken. The wood nymph was free to go.

Harold's bit of daring-do had left him a changed man. Well, that and talking to me eye-to-eye. He left the stage holding the wood nymph's hand to waves of thunderous applause. I'm not sure what the audience was expecting, but an action/adventure/love story probably wasn't it.

While Harold was making his exit to much-deserved applause, I tried to sneak off stage. Diz grabbed my hand instead, and we took a deep, theatrical bow, center stage.

"Why did you do that?" I asked him as we made our way back to the car.

He grinned at me. "It's not every day we get a round of applause for doing the right thing."

The sight of one of Diz's rare, honest-to-goodness grins went a good long way to chasing away the residual butterflies in my stomach. Have I mentioned how terrified I am of being on stage?

"We didn't do all that much," I said. "Harold deserves the credit here. He must have followed Blackthorne to the theater, then concocted a plan with the chloroform."

I shook my head, remembering the way Harold and the wood nymph had left the stage, hand in hand. Harold's old high school crush was a lot more than just a crush. No one in the family had realized that the wood nymph was the love of Harold's life. No wonder Harold had been so devastated by what Blackthorne had done to him all those years ago. I hoped everything worked out right for them from here on out.

"True," Diz said.

"At least my mother will be happy." My mother and my aunt. I'd made Harold promise to call his mother right away and to never disappear like that again.

But if Diz agreed with me that we didn't do much,

why the curtain call bow? "I still don't get it," I said. "Why did you make me take a bow?"

An expression stole over Diz's face that made him look suspiciously like my cat when she thinks she's pulled one over on me. "The only way to beat a nightmare is to face it down," he said.

I stopped dead in my tracks, my mouth hanging open.

How did Diz know about my nightmare?

"You talk in your sleep," he said to my unasked question.

I clamped my mouth shut. Diz and I didn't sleep together. We've never slept together. Trust me, I'd remember something like that.

Although I may have dozed off at my desk once or twice. Or on the loveseat in the front office. I'm usually not that sound of a sleeper, but Diz can be a stealthy elf when he wants to be. What else did I say when I didn't know I was talking, much less know I had an audience? Nightmares aren't the only kind of dreams I've had at the office.

Diz chuckled as we walked the rest of the way back to the car. I tried not to blush, but I'm pretty sure I wasn't too successful.

I really need to get my partner a bell.

A loud one.

GOBBLER, GOBBLER, WHO'S GOT THE GOBBLER?

I answered my cell phone two days before Thanksgiving, and my mother said, "Someone stole my turkey!"

Okay, not what I was expecting.

I'd answered my phone without thinking because I was waiting for a call from my partner. Diz, the better half of Diz & Dee Investigations, had taken his gorgeous but grumpy elf self down to the docks to meet with an informant from the days when we'd both been cops.

Diz still kept in touch with most of his informants. I'd never had any to begin with. When you're a human woman with a touch of precognition, most of the criminal fringe element tend to avoid you like the plague. I'm sure they thought I could pick up on all their dirty little secrets, but that's not how my precog visions work.

When they work. Which is rarely when I want them to.

So by the time my brain registered the fact that the

ringtone was the shower scene music from *Psycho* that I'd assigned to my mother's cell phone number instead of the nifty little jazz riff I'd assigned to Diz's cell—he was named after Dizzy Gillespie, after all—it was too late to simply let my mother's call roll over to voicemail.

Not that I've ever done that.

That I'll admit to.

"Your turkey," I said to my mother. "You're calling me about your missing turkey."

I shouldn't have been surprised that my mother called me because something had gone missing. She seems to think I have a magic crystal ball in my head and I can find anything that goes missing, from her car keys all the way to my cousin Harold.

Although Diz and I did find Harold. The car keys? Not so much.

"Not missing," she said. "Stolen."

"That sucks," I said. "But can't you just go buy another one?"

Yes, it was two days before Thanksgiving, and yes, I'd been avoiding grocery shopping for a week because I'm allergic to standing in long checkout lines while house-wives pass judgment on my lifestyle based on the donuts, celery, and tuna in my cart. (The tuna's for my cat.) But still, all the stores couldn't be sold out of turkeys already, could they?

"No," my mother said. "Simpkins is not that kind of turkey. He's a rescue turkey."

A rescue turkey. Did I hear that right? There were

really such things as rescue turkeys? And she'd named hers Simpkins?

"He's a very nice bird." My mother sniffled. "He was rescued from a poultry hoarder. Didn't you hear about it on the news? Horrible conditions, even by poultry farm standards."

It was too early in the morning for this. It didn't matter that it was nearly ten o'clock, that I'd already finished both of my morning cups of coffee and half of the second donut I'd allowed myself (it was two days before Thanksgiving, after all, and I could always cut back after the holidays were over), and I'd just put the finishing touches on a status report for our current (and only) client. It was still too early in the morning to consider things like rescue turkeys and poultry hoarders.

"If he's a very nice bird," I said, pinching the bridge of my nose between my thumb and forefinger, "do you think his former owner just came to take him back?"

"The hoarder's in jail." My mother sniffled again. "He wasn't a very nice man, Dee. Poor Simpkins. I wish I could have rescued all the turkeys, but I was only allowed to adopt one of those poor birds. Can't you just come out and do your thing so I can bring Simpkins home? I'm so worried that someone's going to do something terrible to him, with the holiday and all."

Do my thing.

I wished it was that easy. I've never been able to convince my mother that I have no conscious control over my visions, but now wasn't the time to remind her of that fact. She sounded really upset. How would I feel if someone stole my cat right before a holiday where roast cat was number one on the menu?

I have a cat. My mother has a turkey. We all love what we love.

"I'll be right over," I said and clicked off the call.

Before I left the office, I placed a call to Diz's cell. The call rang right over to voicemail. Diz has an annoying habit—one of many—of turning off his phone when he's out in the field, especially when he's meeting with informants. It's a good thing he's so gorgeous.

Not that I'd ever tell him that.

"I'm going to my mother's," I said to his voicemail. "Call me when you get a chance." I almost hung up before I added, "Oh, and you might want to check with your informants to see if anyone's heard about a black market turkey ring."

It was a long shot, but hey, we lived in Moretown Bay. We've seen stranger things than that.

MY MOM and dad still live in the house where I grew up in an area of Moretown Bay known as Merlin Heights.

Merlin Heights is one of those cookie cutter suburban subdivisions that was built in the days when home-owners associations were still just a glimmer in housing developers' eyes, so pretty much anything goes. The houses are all laid out the same—living room in front, kitchen in the back, and a tiny dining room in between. The only difference is whether the house has two moderate-sized bedrooms or three dinky ones, and whether the garage was meant to hold one car or two.

That's where the similarities end.

Thanks to not having to abide by any rigid, predetermined community standards, the houses were all painted a wild variety of colors—my parents' house is a soft-toned teal with an off-white trim—with front yards as unique as the people who lived inside.

The widow down the street had painted her house the color pink usually found only in a bottle of liquid antacid, and the trim is lime green. She does tarot readings for my mother and the other women in the neighborhood. The widow's yard is filled with neatly trimmed shrubs and flowers and about a bazillion garden gnomes. Statues, not real ones.

I'm told real gnomes find the statues funny, not offensive. I think they must have stock in the company that makes them.

The neighbor across the street from my parents' house is a metalwork artist. His house is brown, the trim dark green, and his front yard is crammed full of whimsical metal whirligigs and doodads. My mother says that for an extra fifty bucks, he'll etch decorative designs into his creations. I doubt the designs are purely decorative but are more on the order of runes and sigils, but my mother tends to ignore the magical aspects of life unless they smack her in the face.

Or she needs my help.

My parents' house has three dinky bedrooms and a two-car garage. It also has a lawn in the front, my old swing set in the back that they're keeping for the grand-children I've yet to give them, and a hand-painted sign tacked on to the front yard fence that reads, "Havc you seen this bird?" complete with an 8x10 color photo of a brown-feathered turkey that had to be Simpkins.

Not a bad-looking bird. For a turkey.

The garage door was open when I arrived, and I found my dad inside.

I don't think my parents' car has ever seen the inside of their garage. My dad turned the garage into a work-shop before I was born, long before the term "man cave" became popular.

And yes, my parents have always had a car. They live in the suburbs. I live in the city. I used to have a car, but I can barely afford the rent on my apartment. When my car threw some little part into some bigger part that meant something major no longer worked, the repair estimate was more than I could afford. I had no choice but to let my car go to that great scrapheap south of town.

Which means I'm currently car-less. That's okay most of the time because Diz has a car. A nice car. When-ever we actually need to drive ourselves somewhere, Diz does the driving and I ride shotgun.

Except when Diz is off doing one of his "elf things" and I need to go somewhere beyond walking distance. Then I call a car service.

Still cheaper than trying to fix my own car.

I'd called a car service today to drop me off at my parents' house. At least this time my driver was a full-sized goblin who thankfully didn't believe banter short-ened the drive. The last time I took a car service out to my parents' house, the driver had been a gnome perched on a booster seat who'd controlled the car with a touch-screen monitor. She'd talked my ear off.

At least until she'd seen the widow's garden gnomes. "That one looks like my cousin Stan," she'd said. "I never did like Stan."

That particular garden gnome was brandishing a garden trowel like a serial killer holding a butcher knife and had a demented smile on its little plastic face.

I don't think I would have liked her cousin Stan either.

"You really need your own car," my dad said in greeting after the goblin pulled away. "How can you be an investigator if you don't have a car? How can you go follow leads? Isn't that what you call it?"

The pull-down light over my dad's workbench was on. Several cans of things were open, and I could smell varnish and paint thinner and the dusty hot smell of an electric heater doing its best to keep the damp chill of the morning off whatever Dad had been working on. Prob-ably the missing-turkey sign in the front yard.

"That's what I call it," I said. "And the office does have a car. It's Diz's car, and he needed it this morning. I was just supposed to be doing paperwork."

Plus, a good deal of the investigating we do can be done on the internet. You don't need a car for that, but I didn't mention that to my dad. He's actually kind of proud that I own my own business, and that the business helps find missing people.

My dad harrumphed at me, then he gave me a brief hug.

Somewhere over the years my dad went from being the biggest man in my life to being this medium-sized, compact older guy only an inch or so taller than I am who had a full head of steel gray hair and faded green eyes. He'd worked pretty much his entire life until a couple of years ago when he was "encouraged" to take early retirement. Now he putters in his work space in the garage—doing what, I'm never really sure of—but retirement seems to agree with him.

I always got the impression that for the most part my dad was a pretty easy-going, happy guy, even after a handful of decades living with my mother. But not this morning. I could tell by the worry lines at the corners of his eyes.

"She's really upset, huh," I said.

"That bird's her baby. We're not even having turkey for Thanksgiving this year. Ham. That's what she's cooking. A ham. God knows what we'll have for holiday dinners if she ever rescues a pig."

"What about the stuffing?" I asked. "How's she going to cook that?"

"Pineapple," Dad said. "She says pineapple goes with ham, not stuffing."

I blinked. My mother's stuffing was legendary. I'd tried to replicate her recipe over the years, but I'd never even come close. Not that I'm the world's greatest cook to begin with, but some things are just tradition.

"Cranberry sauce?" I asked. My mom always made her own cranberry sauce too.

"Nope," Dad said with a sigh. "Just pineapple. And some sort of roasted vegetables."

The door connecting the garage to the house swung open. "Is he complaining about the menu again?" my mother asked. "You'd think I'd committed a crime the way he's been complaining."

My dad didn't complain. My mother's sister Gloria complained pretty much non-stop. Mom probably got the two of them confused. My Aunt Gloria has a mustache that looks remarkably like my dad's except my dad's has more gray and he keeps his neatly trimmed.

My mother stepped down the two concrete steps from the house to the garage. The aroma of fresh-brewed coffee followed her out the door, and my stomach rumbled.

Normally my mother would start off every conversation by telling me I'm too thin, I'm not eating right, and then she'd offer to make me a healthy breakfast of bacon and eggs scrambled with shredded cheese. My stomach had anticipated the offer—my mom manages to cook the bacon just right every single time—but she surprised me by getting right to the point.

"Have you had any visions?" she asked. "Do you know who took Simpkins?" She sniffled. "He's not in anyone's oven, is he?" She looked over my shoulder. "And where's your partner?"

My mother might not understand how my visions work—to be honest, I'm not all that sure why I even have visions in the first place, they're so unreliable—but she's definitely on Team Diz. I actually think she might have a little crush on him, but since I happen to have my share of not-workplace-appropriate fantasies about my partner, I try not to think too much about that.

The fact that she'd mentioned her turkey first instead of Diz went to show just how worried she was about her rescue bird. It was two days to Thanksgiving. If anything, Simpkins might be in someone's refrigerator, not their oven, but I wasn't about to tell my mother that. I wouldn't want to hear that my cat might be in someone's refrigerator awaiting "the big day."

"Not yet," I said. "It might help if you tell me a little more about Simpkins."

We went into the house and my mother made me a delicious single-serve cup of coffee from a shiny new gadget on the kitchen counter.

My mother loves her kitchen gadgets. She usually gives me one for Christmas or my birthday, but I have no idea how to use most of them so they stay in the box. If she gave me one of the coffee-making gadgets for Christmas this year, I'd certainly be motivated to figure it out.

While the three of us sat at my parents' dining room table, currently decorated with a Hawaiian-themed silk flower arrangement, my mother told me about Simpkins.

Simpkins had started off life as a free-range bird on a farm in the eastern part of the state. "He's not one of those big-breasted birds," my mother said. "And he's got brown feathers, not white like those poor birds who are kept penned up in tiny cages. That's what the hoarder did with him. Kept him in one of those little cages. That's just cruel. You should have seen the state of his feathers when I first brought him home."

I wasn't a fan of big-breasted turkeys either, but that was because I never knew what to do with all the leftover breast meat. I'm more of a drumstick fan myself.

"How did he end up with the hoarder?" I asked.

"The farm went belly up," my dad said. "He was sold to the highest bidder at auction."

And the highest bidder had been the turkey hoarder.

"He brought a pretty penny," my mother said with more than a hint of pride. "He's a special bird."

I looked at my dad. He gave me a raised eyebrow.

Okay, I'll bite.

"What's so special about Simpkins?" I asked.

My mother leaned over the table like she was about to tell me a state secret.

"He can fly," she said.

It's a popular myth that turkeys can't fly.

Well, most domesticated turkeys, the big-breasted ones, can't really fly. It has something to do with power-to-mass ratio and other scientific things I don't pretend to understand.

I'd used my cell phone to do some quick research on

turkeys during the car ride over to my parents' house. The bottom line was that domesticated turkeys can't flap their wings fast enough to get their oversized, big-breasted bodies off the ground except for extremely short bursts.

Not being a big-breasted turkey, Simpkins didn't have that problem. It didn't make him all that special. Wild turkeys can fly. In fact, they're pretty darn fast over short distances.

"So," I asked my mother slowly, cupping my hands around my delicious cup of coffee. "Do you think he just flew away?"

"Oh, he wouldn't do that," my mother said quickly. "He likes me. He knows I wouldn't cook him for Thanksgiving dinner. We're having ham."

I didn't point out that she'd cooked turkey for Thanksgiving dinners for as long as I could remember. Not that Simpkins knew that.

"How do you know he likes you?" I asked.

One thing I had noticed during my research was the small size of a turkey's brain. I figured their likes and dislikes boiled down to who fed them, who didn't eat them, and which hen turkey looked especially hot on a Saturday night.

"I give him the best food," my mother said. "I rescued him from the man who kept him in a really small cage. And I sing to him every morning before the fog burns away so he doesn't get frightened."

"The hoarder's place was down by the bay," my dad explained. "The farm where he was raised didn't get fog, just a little morning mist. He has a bit of post-traumatic stress whenever the fog rolls in."

Moretown Bay has fog almost every morning since the city's right next to the bay it's named for. The nearly constant fog and cloud cover is why I don't try to do anything with my hair that could remotely be called "styling." The closest I get is pulling the curly mess into a pony tail, like I had that morning.

"So are you getting any visions yet?" my mother asked. "Do you know who took my bird?"

My precog abilities were still annoyingly silent. Maybe they could use another cup of coffee.

"How about I show you where Simpkins lives?" my mother asked. "Would that help?"

My precog visions don't usually show up just because I've touched something owned by whoever's missing, but it certainly wouldn't hurt. "Lead the way," I said to my mother.

In addition to my old swing set, my parents' back yard has a cherry tree, an apple tree, and a few shrubs that flower just enough in the springtime to make my dad sneeze. Like most of the yards in the neighborhood, it's barely big enough to hold all those things plus my dad's barbecue and the two lawn chairs sitting in a patch of grass that looked like it was hanging on for dear life, but my parents have always made it work.

Now the yard also sported a watering trough big enough for a small child to use as a wading pool, and a section of the lawn looked like it had been raked over by a demented garden gnome, just like one of the statues down the street.

"That's where I feed Simpkins," my mother said, pointing at the ravaged section of grass. "I sit in my chair in the morning before the fog burns off and I sing to him, and he always talks back to me." She sighed. "It's so nice, hearing his gobbles in the fog."

"It's not nice, it's creepy," my dad said. "Hearing disembodied gobbles in the fog."

"That's only because you haven't gotten to know him," my mother said.

Personally I thought it was because my dad had always wanted a dog but he got a turkey instead. My mother claimed she was allergic to dog hair. Apparently she wasn't allergic to turkey feathers.

There were a few turkey feathers stuck in the lawn near where Simpkins got his morning serenades from my mother. Large brown feathers that were far prettier than turkey feathers had a right to be.

I bent over to pick up one of the feathers. It was about as long as my hand and stiffer than I expected. I reminded myself that people used to make quill pens out of bird feathers, and then I tried to imagine writing with the sharpened tip of a turkey feather.

Then I wondered if Diz had ever written with a bird feather quill. For all I knew, it could be one of his elf things.

Like climbing up the side of a building like it was an over-sized tree instead of waiting for the elevator. Or having perfect balance. Or—

The world around me started to gray out.

The morning fog had already burned away out here in Merlin Heights and there were only regular clouds overhead, so I was pretty sure this was the start of an actual vision. I hoped it was about Simpkins since I was still holding the turkey feather, but for all I knew, I could be getting a vision about Stan, the maniacal, trowel-wielding gnome.

Then my cell phone rang. A nifty little jazz number that erupted out of the pocket of my jeans, and for the first time in my life, the vision stopped before it even got up a good head of steam.

"You have horrible timing," I said to my partner when I answered the call.

"I've been doing some checking into that black market turkey thing," he said, "and I think we need to talk."

Amazing how when Diz said "black market turkey thing," it didn't sound weird at all.

"Where are you?" he asked.

"I'm still at my parents' house. I almost had a vision, but it's gone now." I shoved the turkey feather in my jacket pocket, more frustrated than normal at my lack of control over my visions.

"Stay there," he said. "I'm on my way."

He hung up, and I looked at my parents' expectant faces.

"We might have a lead," I said.

I just hoped it wasn't to where we could pick up a really good turkey dinner.

145

D<small>IZ</small> GREW up on Marlette Island in the middle of the bay. He comes from a long line of wood elves who spend their time caring for the forest and the creatures they share the island with, and who basically live quiet, contemplative lives among the trees.

Diz isn't quiet or contemplative. He's not slender or blond or serene like the elves in those movies. He's built like The Rock before The Rock became known as Dwayne Johnson, movie star, and he has the glower and one-eyebrow-lifted intense stare that goes with it. Diz has shoulder-length hair the color of cinnamon with a few marshmallow highlights thrown in here and there. At least his hair's shoulder length in the back. He cuts it short on the sides and on the top, probably to show off his ears, but that means he wears a mullet.

Nobody—and I mean *nobody*—gives him a hard time about that mullet.

Diz is dazzlingly gorgeous and strong and sure of foot like most elves, and like most elves, he's a lot older than he looks. Diz left the island when he was much younger— probably around the time teenage me had her first precog vision—and joined the magical division of the Moretown Bay Police Department. By the time my precog ability got me a promotion to the detective bureau and an assignment as his partner in the Bureau of Magical Enforcement, Diz was a seasoned cop while I was still pretty much a rookie.

When I left the force to open my own detective

agency, he decided to join me. I'm still not one-hundred percent sure why.

He's not as bad-tempered these days as he was when he was on the force, although he's still almost always grumpy. Except when he's around my cat, who adores him. My cat has good taste.

He also has the most adorable pointy ears that I've always longed to touch. Among other things, but that's something reserved for my fantasies.

So far. But a girl can hope.

Diz showed up twenty minutes later driving his sporty black car. He must have saved a lot of money over the years while he was on the force because he certainly couldn't afford a car like that on the money the agency makes. It's something else I don't ask about. He'd probably just tell me it's "an elf thing."

My parents came out front with me when he pulled up.

"Have you found Simpkins?" my mother asked, leaning down to talk to Diz through the open window of his car.

Diz arched an eyebrow at me. He does a better eyebrow arch than my father.

"The turkey," I explained. "He's a special bird."

"He's why we're having ham for Thanksgiving," my dad added.

Diz grunted. "I might have a lead," he said as I let myself in the passenger side of the car.

"I'll call you," I told my mother. "Try not to worry."

Once we'd pulled away from my parents' house, I turned to Diz. "Should she worry?" I asked.

"It depends on how much she likes that bird," he said.

That didn't sound good. "Tell me what you found out," I said. "What are we dealing with?"

"Not a black market ring," he said. "A cult."

Cult? Now I did the eyebrow arch. "A turkey cult?"

"A sacrificial turkey cult," he said. "At least in the states. In other countries, cult members sacrifice other animals and then have a feast. It's an indigenous thing."

"Native Americans?" I asked.

He gave me a brief negative shake of his head. "Indigenous magic folk. Certain fringe elements perform ritual animal sacrifices on whatever holiday is traditionally meant to give thanks for hearth and home."

If you looked at it like that, everyone did something similar when they celebrated Thanksgiving with their friends and family. Most of us just didn't kill the main course ourselves.

I mentioned that to Diz. "So what makes that a cult?" I asked. "Besides killing the turkey themselves before they cook it?"

At least I assumed they cooked it. Some magic folk, like goblins, preferred their food raw. Or rotten.

"Other than spilling blood into the earth," he said, "which I'm sure your parents don't do, the whole purpose behind the ritual is to ask the earth to send the invaders home."

Oh.

Magic folk have been around far longer than mortals. These days most magic folk have assimilated into the "real" world. Even the old gods, like Eros, run businesses instead of relying on tithes and offerings. By "invaders," I had no doubt the cultists were trying to send vanilla mortals—like my parents—back to wherever they came from.

Which, in this case, was Poughkeepsie.

Unless that wasn't far enough.

"They want to eradicate all mortals?" I asked. "Can they actually do that?"

Diz shrugged one muscular shoulder. "Magic is tricky. If they got ahold of the right sacrifice? Or enough of them did it all at once?"

He gave me a look that said "who knows?"

I suppressed a shiver. My mother had said Simpkins was special. What if he was the right sacrifice that would make the ritual actually work?

If he'd been bird-napped by turkey-sacrificing cultists, at least the good news was that he might still be alive. The bad news was cultists could be a little unhinged. Especially cultists who wielded magic.

"So where are we going?" I asked as Diz turned the car in the direction of South Bay.

"My source gave me the name of a bakery where the local cultists buy pies for the ritual."

I blinked. "Pies?"

"Everybody likes pie," he said.

∽

149

WE DIDN'T GO ALL the way to South Bay, which made me breathe a sigh of relief.

South Bay houses some shady businesses in the acres and acres of warehouses and light industrial factories. But between South Bay and the residential suburbs that surround the southern end of Moretown Bay proper lies an area of businesses and restaurants that cater to the hipster chic. Whole food eateries, specialty cheese shops, gourmet coffee importers, and clothing stores featuring fashions made from natural fibers only.

Tucked into these businesses in an old converted residential two-story house was Pretty Polly's Perfect Pies and Pastries. That's where Diz's informant said the cultists bought the desserts for their annual ritual turkey sacrifice.

I didn't have to open the door of the shop to know this was a quality bakery. The memory of that morning's delicious donuts couldn't hold a candle to the mouth-watering aroma surrounding the building like a sugary sweet cloud. Cinnamon-spiced apples, honeyed peaches, and tangy sweet lemons competed with the buttery goodness of pastries flakey enough to melt in your mouth.

I think I might actually have groaned.

Diz gave me a sideways glance, and I could swear one side of his mouth twitched in what passed for a smile. "Hungry?" he asked.

"My mother didn't feed me," I said in my defense.

It was a few minutes before one in the afternoon by the time we made it to Pretty Polly's, but the place was still packed to the gills with people picking up their holiday pastries. This was probably Polly's busiest time of the year.

Except there was no Polly.

By the time the crowd thinned and we made it to the counter, I could see the bakery was staffed entirely with gnomes.

Male gnomes.

Bearded male gnomes wearing white pointed hats. The gnomes walked back and forth along a platform behind the counter that raised them up to nearly eye level with their customers, most of whom at least looked human.

"Can I help you?" one of the gnomes asked.

He had a semi-demented look on that chubby, round face of his. It could have been the crush of holiday customers—most of the bakers here probably hadn't had much sleep in the last week or so—but I could imagine this particular gnome wielding a garden trowel. Or a butcher knife.

"Your name wouldn't happen to be Stan, would it?" I asked.

He narrowed his eyes at me. "Who wants to know?"

I introduced myself and Diz. "If your name's Stan," I said, "I think I met your cousin."

"Ingrid," he said, shaking his head. "She drives for one of those car services, right?"

I hadn't known my driver's name, but I nodded my head anyway.

"Great scam that company's got going," Stan said.

"Pay's shitty, and they make you drive your own car. But Ingrid's never worn the sharpest hat in the family."

Apparently insulting a gnome's hat was the ultimate insult among other gnomes. I'd have to remember that.

"So what can I get you fine folks today?" Stan asked.

Next to me, Diz balled one hand into a loose fist.

That was his signal that he sensed magic at work. Not the everyday kind of magic, but the kind of magic that utilized spells and potions and other things that might be a tad on the illegal or dangerous side.

Like most elves, Diz can sense when that kind of magic is in play. It helped us catch a lot of bad guys when we were cops, and it helps us find a lot of missing people (and things, and hopefully one missing turkey) now that we're in the private sector. It meant that someone in Pretty Polly's was using magic.

Or someone who'd been in Polly's recently had been using magic.

I didn't think Diz would signal me if he only sensed enhancement magic, the kind that would rev up the smell of baked goods or the flavor of Pretty Polly's pies. Something else was going on here. But it wasn't strong enough that we'd need backup from a wizard of our own. Diz's fist would have been clenched much tighter if that had been the case.

"We're not really in the market for pies," I said, although I wouldn't mind trying one of their apple pies. There were a few on display in the case, and they looked like something I'd want to make an entire meal of, not just save for dessert. "We're more in the market for information."

Stan's chubby face went carefully blank. "What kind of information?"

Diz leaned forward just the slightest bit and glowered at Stan.

Stan swallowed audibly, but he stood his ground. My estimation of his character went up a notch from potential trowel-wielding serial killer to determined trowel-wielding baker. I've seen hardened criminals melt into a puddle of goo when subjected to my partner's glower.

"We're looking for a turkey," Diz said, all business. "You wouldn't happen to know anything about that, would you?"

"It's my mother's turkey," I said. "She's pretty upset."

"She can't just buy another one at the grocer's?" Stan asked.

"It's not that kind of a bird," Diz said. "It's a very special turkey."

"Oh," Stan said. He swallowed again.

It was pretty clear Stan knew exactly what we were talking about. I gave him a few beats to decide whether to be more afraid of Diz or the cultists. I'd bet my money on Diz.

Stan finally leaned forward and lowered his voice. "They're crazy. If they know I've talked to you, they'll have *me* on the chopping block next year."

"Not if we can prove they kidnapped my mother's turkey with intent to practice a little malevolent magic," I said.

In Moretown Bay, like in most of the country, casting unlicensed spells could you cited and fined. Practicing ritual animal sacrifice for the purpose of performing a spell that would send all mortals back to where they came could get you thrown in prison behind magic-dampening bars for the rest of your life. The wizards in charge of enforcing the law on magic folk take their jobs very, very seriously, and Diz and I still had contacts in the police department.

"Oh," Stan said again.

He looked over his shoulder, and then stood on tiptoes to look over our shoulders. Once he was satisfied we were the only ones in the shop that could hear him, he started talking, and fast.

"We only make pies, you understand," he said. "We can't control who buys them or what they use them for. But a few years ago this guy started coming in. Ex-hippy looking, mostly human, but with a definite flare about him, you know?"

"Magic," Diz said.

"Yes, but it had a wild taste to it, like he couldn't control it without a little help," Stan said.

I raised an eyebrow. Apparently gnomes, or at least this gnome, could sense magic too. Good to know.

"He told me his 'group' needed a few pies for their annual get together, and every year he gives me these pie pans he wants me to use. He said he made them himself special for their group." Stan shrugged. "We get our pie pans custom made from a company in South Bay, they've got our logo stamped into the bottom and they're reusable so anytime anybody uses one to make a pie, they think about how good ours were, you know? Advertising."

"Get to the point," Diz growled.

Stan trembled visibly. "Yeah. Okay. So this guy brings back the pie pans every year, and every time I notice he's got something etched into the bottom and along the edges, but it's always different, year to year."

"A logo?" I asked.

Stan shook his head. "More like something to channel his magic, if you ask me, but I'm no expert. I only make pies. He was in here about an hour ago to pick up this year's pies."

In pans with symbols etched in the metal to help channel magic.

"Runes and sigils," I said.

"That would be my guess," Diz said.

Etched in metal.

That couldn't be a coincidence. Sure, more than one metal artist lived in the city, but there was only one metal artist who knew exactly where he could get his hands on a live turkey—my mother's live turkey—two days before Thanksgiving. A live turkey that was more wild than domesticated, just like his magic.

"I think we need to head back to my parents' house," I told Diz. "We need to have a talk with their neighbor."

Have I mentioned that my precog visions are a tad unreliable? A touch unpredictable?

We were on my way back to my mother's house when the world around me abruptly disappeared and I found myself on a dirt floor breathing in sharply scented, smoky air.

Sometimes my visions let me piggyback on someone else's experience—or, more precisely, the experience someone else is about to have at some undetermined point in the future. In those visions, I can only see what that person sees, which can be annoyingly unhelpful if that person doesn't look in the right direction to give me at least a clue as to where they are.

At other times, I simply get a whiff of something smelly or a flash of something seen out of the corner of my eye. Those visions are the least helpful of all, unless the flash of something seen out of the corner of my eye is something someone's misplaced. That never worked with my mother's keys, though it did work the one time my Aunt Gloria left her reading glasses at the checkout counter in the grocery store.

Then there are times, like this one, when I'm more of a ghostly observer of something that's going to—or might—happen in the future unless I do something to change it.

At least in these visions I can usually look around if I concentrate hard enough.

The problem with this vision was there was nothing much really to look at other than a dirt floor and the inside of what looked like a very normal, very dark garden shed.

I did see shadowy shapes of trowels and rakes and a shovel. A lawnmower crouched in one corner, and along with the smoky air I could smell recently cut grass. The bag for the lawnmower hung on a hook off the ceiling next to other shapes I couldn't quite make out, but what could have been machetes or other long-bladed tools. What had to be a can of gasoline for the lawnmower sat on the dirt floor not far from my nose.

I concentrated harder and forced ghostly me to push herself upright. The dark shed swam in my vision for a moment before the world righted itself again and my ghostly vision adjusted to the dark.

In the far corner I could see what we'd been looking for. A large, dark shape of a bird slumped in an ungainly heap.

Simpkins.

But was he still alive?

His head was still attached, which I took to be a good sign, but his eyes were closed and he wasn't moving.

I couldn't tell if he was breathing, so I gritted my ghostly teeth and tried to get closer. As I did, one of his feet twitched and then his toes clenched before they relaxed again.

That was a good sign, right?

At least I knew Simpkins was alive and being held in a tool shed, and the lawnmower meant the shed was more than likely somewhere in the suburbs, but where?

The door to the shed was shut tight. I'd never tried to

pass through walls before during a ghostly vision, but there was a first time for everything. The tool shed was wood, not metal, so that might help. I remembered my mother's anguish at losing her turkey, and I tried to use that to help me concentrate.

Go through the wall, Dee, I told my ghostly self. *You can do it. You can—*

Slam face first into a magical barrier.

Pain flared through my head as a flashbulb-bright light seared my brain, and just like that I was back in Diz's car headed for my parents' house.

I must have gasped because when I opened my eyes, I saw that Diz had pulled into the breakdown lane on the freeway and was staring intently at me.

"I'm okay," I managed to croak out.

I'd slumped against the passenger door as far as my seatbelt would allow. I scooted around until I was sitting upright again. A doozy of a headache was catching its second wind behind my eyeballs, and my stomach felt like Stan the gnome had marched around inside with his shiny black boots, hacking away at my guts with a garden trowel.

"You don't look okay," Diz said. "Vision?"

"Yeah." And a weird one at that. "Good news is that Simpkins is still alive. He's out cold, either drugged or spelled, and he's locked inside a tool shed in someone's backyard."

"And the bad news?" Diz asked.

I rubbed my forehead with the heel of one hand. "I

have no idea where the shed is, and to top it off, the thing's warded to high heaven."

"I'm not surprised," Diz said. "Whoever owns that shed's planning to perform an illegal ritual with a stolen bird. The wards might be keeping your mother's turkey knocked out. Tell me more about your vision."

Diz merged back into traffic as I told him as much as I could remember about the vision. How dark it was, all the shadowy tools I could see, what I smelled, and Simpkins in a heap in one corner.

"What time of day?" Diz asked.

"Night," I said automatically, but then I paused.

I'd thought it was night because the inside of the shed was so dark. But how had I seen any of the tools—or Simpkins for that matter—if the shed had been totally dark? Ghostly me doesn't have any better night vision than real-life me.

I hadn't seen a window in the shed, but there'd been a door.

And light had been filtering in around the edges of the door. Not daylight, thought. Flickering light, like—

"Fire," I said. "There was a fire outside, that's why I could smell smoke."

Diz grunted. "That makes sense. Spill the blood of the sacrifice into the dirt, and then cook it and eat it."

"On Thanksgiving," I said. "That's two days from now." Usually my visions didn't give me that much of a heads-up.

Something about that fire niggled at the back of my brain. Something about the smell.

The inside of the shed had been ripe with smells. I haven't had all that many ghostly visions, but when I do, the sights and sounds—and smells—are usually muted, which I always figured was because my ghostly self wasn't altogether present in whatever the vision was showing me. But what I'd smelled in the shed had been sharp if not immediately recognizable.

I'd seen the lawnmower and the gas can, so my brain had filled in those scents. But had that been what I'd really smelled? Or was it something else? Something that should have been familiar. Would have been familiar if I actually still lived in my parents' house.

I'm a city girl now. City smells, I'm familiar with. The scent of rain on concrete, of walking past a full garbage can on pickup day, or the smell of Korean barbeque venting from the roof of the restaurant down the street. Even the scent of the aroma therapy candles wafting out the open door of the masseuse's shop across the street from our office on a hot afternoon.

But the scent in my vision was something out of my childhood. Back when I got home from school on a late fall afternoon, and my dad had been raking leaves and hauled an old metal trash can out front and—

"Burning leaves!" I blurted out. "Not a sacrificial fire, but burning leaves. That's what I smelled!"

And not only burning leaves, but the same kind of burning leaves I'd smelled in my childhood. A mixture of apple leaves and cherry leaves and pine needles that blew in our yard from the big tree next door.

My parents' house wasn't the only one in the neighborhood with fruit trees in the backyard. I now had a pretty good idea whose backyard had a warded shed containing one stolen Thanksgiving turkey.

My mother's friend, the tarot card reading widow down the street.

The one with the demented garden gnomes guarding her front yard.

STATUES CAN BE JUST STATUES, but they can also be early warning devices if they're spelled properly.

Diz balled one hand into a loose fist when we got out of the car in front of the widow's house, signaling that he felt low-level magic in use.

My stomach still hadn't quite recovered from the after-effects from my vision, and just looking at that pink house, complete with neon lime green trim, wasn't help-ing. My insides gurgled ominously as we approached the front gate. The garden gnomes inside all seemed to be glaring at me with their black plastic painted eyes.

"Warded?" I asked as I reached for the latch. I didn't see a warning sign or even a No Trespassing sign, but I thought I ask to be on the safe side.

"No," Diz said. "Feels more on the order of a doorbell spell."

The magical equivalent of a motion sensor, either embedded into the yard's white picket fence or in the more demented-looking gnomes that lined the sidewalk leading to the front door.

Diz avoided the front gate by leaping gracefully over the fence and landing halfway down the widow's front walk. He didn't immediately leap out of the yard or grab his head in pain or even wince, which I took as a good sign.

Not having even a smidgen of his elvish grace, I unlatched the gate and let myself in. All I felt was a slight static charge when I shut the gate behind myself.

By the time we reached the widow's front porch, where we were surrounded by even more garden gnomes, the widow had her front door open.

Doorbell spell. My partner had been right.

"Dee!" she said with genuine pleasure. "How nice to see you. I haven't seen you in the neighborhood in years, it seems like."

She still looked like the same sweet little old lady I remembered from my childhood. Shorter than my mother, rounder than my mother, with wispy white hair surrounding a pleasantly round face. She had more wrinkles now, of course, and she leaned on a cane as she stood inside her front door. The scent of cinnamon, nutmeg, and cloves wafting from her kitchen only barely masked the damp smell of fallen leaves from the cherry trees and apple trees that shared space with a huge pine tree in the corner of her back yard.

I introduced Diz, who surprised me by taking the widow's outstretched hand (the one not holding her cane) and bending over it in a slight bow. The widow tittered and color rose in her cheeks.

"My," she said when Diz released her hand. "What a sweet young man, your friend is."

I hadn't introduced Diz as my partner. I was hoping we could keep this visit as friendly as possible, so when she invited us in for tea, I accepted.

She proceeded us into the kitchen, although I knew where it would be since her house was laid out inside just like the one my parents lived in.

As he passed me, Diz whispered, "It's not her," into my ear. "The spells are all purchased."

I tried not to shiver when his lips brushed against my ear, and I definitely tried not to think about how amazing it would be to whisper into his pointy ears. Not that I would ever need to be that close to whisper to him. Elves have amazing hearing. Damn it.

As for the spells, Diz has told me that purchased spells all have a certain feel that's woven into the magic. Basically it acts like a manufacturer's logo that can be used to trace a spell back to its source. Homemade spells, for lack of a better term, have no logos attached.

In other words, the widow purchased her doorbell spells from a reputable source. Diz didn't sense any magical ability emanating from the widow herself, which made me wonder about her tarot readings.

The widow's kitchen was bright and cheery, with nary a garden gnome in sight. The walls were painted soft yellow, the windowsills off-white, and the window was trimmed with gingham curtains sporting a whimsical floral border.

The curtains were open, giving us a clear look at her

backyard. There, off to one corner, sat a metal barrel filled with leaves, ready for burning. And about five feet away along the back fence sat a wooden garden shed. Windowless, and with a big new padlock on the door.

"Do you mind if we have a look inside your garden shed?" I asked the widow.

"My garden shed?" she asked, confusion knitting a line between her brows.

"We're looking for my mother's turkey," I said. "He's missing."

The widow looked between me and Diz, who now wore his usual grumpy expression. "Can't she just buy another one at the store? And why would you think her Thanksgiving turkey would be in my shed?"

Clearly the widow didn't know my mother had a real live bird this year. My mother must have been too busy lately singing to Simpkins to have her tarot read.

"Indulge me," I said, giving her my best reassuring smile. Good cop to Diz's grumpy cop.

"Well, I don't..." The widow trailed off, and her shoulders slumped. "I'd really love to help you, but I don't have a key."

"Who does?" I asked.

"Teddy," she said. "He does my yard work these days. It's too hard for me since my hip went bad to bend down and do all that work. I can't even mow my own lawn. Teddy keeps all his tools in the shed, and he locks it up when he's done." She shrugged. "Not that anyone's ever stolen one of my gnomes, but they're his tools, so I don't mind."

"And he didn't give you a spare key?" Diz asked.

The widow shook her head.

"So who's Teddy?" I asked. It hadn't escaped me that she said the name like I should know who that was.

"The nice young man who makes all those metal whirlygigs down the street," she said with a smile. "He's studying to be a wizard, you know."

NICE YOUNG MAN?

Not quite.

Teddy, as it turned out, wasn't even a young man, much less nice.

Theodore Roberts might have been a nice young man at one time, but the Teddy that everyone in my neighborhood knew, that even Stan the baker at Pretty Polly's Perfect Pies and Pastries knew, was a changeling. The changeling had taken over Teddy's identity right down to his metal working abilities when it had moved into the neighborhood seven years ago.

We learned this from the detectives who showed up to arrest Teddy and free Simpkins from the widow's garden shed.

One thing Diz had made me promise when we opened the agency was that if anything smacked of black market magic or something similarly dangerous, we'd call in the police. I had no trouble with that. We'd had some close calls with black magic practitioners when we'd been on the force, and I had no desire to go through that again.

The turkey-sacrificing cult clearly practiced unlicensed magic at the very least, or black magic at the very worst. We called one of our old colleagues at the Bureau of Magical Enforcement, and the police came out to arrest Teddy.

As soon as the police slapped magic-inhibiting handcuffs on him, they'd discovered he was a changeling. The cuffs prevented a changeling from assuming any shape other than their own. The cuffs also cut off a changeling's ability to power any spells, which disabled not only the wards on the widow's garden shed, but also the spell that had been keeping Simpkins safely asleep.

Poor Simpkins. I had no doubt the bird was going to have new post-traumatic issues, but he'd seemed happy enough when he caught sight of my mother. She sang him a lullaby, her eyes shiny bright with unshed tears, and they went off together to my parents' house, Simpkins walking by her side while she had one hand resting lightly on his back.

It turned out the changeling had been studying to increase his magical knowledge. Apparently changeling Teddy had designs on taking over leadership of the local turkey-sacrificing cult, and kidnapping Simpkins to present the bird at this year's ritual would have gone a long way toward replacing the current leader, who always provided store-bought birds for the ritual dinner.

"But what animals did they sacrifice during the ritual?" I asked Diz that night after he got back to the office from the precinct where he'd assisted with interrogating Teddy. Strictly as a civilian consultant, but from the look of satisfaction on his face, Diz had "consulted" quite vigorously—and successfully.

"They didn't," Diz said. He sat down on the loveseat in our front office with the kind of fluid motion that he makes look so simple. "The turkeys were always brined. They dumped the brine in the dirt instead of blood."

"That's why Simpkins was special," I said. He'd actually been a live bird.

The BME investigators had combed through Teddy's house. They found a treasure trove of unlicensed dark magic, including a refrigerator full of pies from Pretty Polly's in the special pans the changeling had spelled. Teddy was going to be spending a lot of years behind magic-inhibiting bars.

My stomach rumbled at the thought of pie. My mother had been so overjoyed to be reunited with Simpkins that she'd sent us each home with half of the ham she'd planned to cook for Thanksgiving.

"I can buy more," she'd said.

I didn't have one clue how to cook ham. I'd have to hit Google and probably go out for a can of pineapple. That didn't help my stomach tonight.

"I need to learn how to make pie," I said. "And maybe cranberry sauce."

One corner of Diz's mouth quirked up in his version of a smile. "Not stuffing?"

I shuddered at the memory of my soggy attempts to

recreate my mother's stuffing. "That doesn't go with ham."

"But cranberry sauce does?"

No, it didn't, but I liked cranberry sauce. Besides, I'd watched my mother made it for years. Cranberries, sugar, and water. How hard could it be?

My cat chose that moment to wander into the office. My apartment is upstairs from the office, and the apartment door came complete with a pet door. I keep the back door to the office open (the door that opens to the stairs), and my cat pretty much has the run of the office as well as my apartment. She likes to sleep on the loveseat in the front office, especially on rare sunny days when the loveseat's nice and warm. She especially likes to sleep on my partner's shoulder.

She hopped up on the loveseat next to Diz then hopped up on his shoulder and rubbed the side of her head on his face before she settled down.

I tried not to give my cat the stink eye. A person shouldn't be jealous of her cat, right?

I loved my cat. My mother loved her turkey. At least my cat didn't have post-traumatic stress. She liked her tuna, and I liked my donuts. She was the perfect roommate. She was just a normal cat who liked doing normal cat things.

In Moretown Bay, things could be far worse.

THE NEW YEAR THAT ALMOST WASN'T

The last person I expected to see walk through my office door on Christmas Eve was one of Santa's elves.

Merry was all of three foot nothing tall. She had green eyes and a cute button nose and her brown curls had grown out since the last time I'd seen her. When we first met the year before, I hadn't realized she was a girl, but there was no mistaking her for a boy this time around. In my defense, back then she'd worn one of the unisex tunics like the rest of the elves. Today she was dressed in a sleeveless red frock and a red Santa hat, and she had cute little gold earrings in her ears.

Merry had been one of a group of elves from the North Pole who'd hired D & D Investigations to find Santa's missing stand-in, Norman. I'm Dee, the human half of D & D Investigations. My partner Diz, the other D in D & D, was out buying a Christmas present for my cat.

Diz and I had agreed not to buy presents for each other this year since the agency was barely staying afloat, and besides, I had no idea what to get a grumpy elf who had everything and always refused to give me a wish list.

"You've got to help me," Merry said in her high-pitched, helium-addict voice. "I'm in big-time trouble."

"Don't tell me Norman's missing again," I said. We'd found Norman easily enough the last time. Finding missing persons was, after all, our specialty, like it said on the sign on our office window, but I had a feeling that if Santa's stand-in had decided to take a powder—again—he'd make himself really scarce this time.

"No." Merry's mouth turned down in a sad little pout. "Baby New Year's mother."

Baby who's what?

"You want to explain that?" I asked.

"Baby New Year." Her eyes narrowed. "You do know who Baby New Year is, right?"

"Short, bald, wears a diaper, a sash, and black top hat, right?" Or at least he did on greeting cards and advertisements, which was all I thought Baby New Year was—somebody's neat advertising gimmick. I should know better by now.

"He's scheduled to be born at midnight on New Year's Eve," Merry said. "They always are, every year, and every year the whole thing runs like clockwork." She sighed. "Except this year."

"When his mother went missing."

"She's the first one who ever ran away, and it's all my fault," Merry said.

I gestured toward one of my pint-sized client chairs. "Why don't you have a seat?"

The last time Merry had been in my office, the only client chairs I had were me-sized, and Santa's elves had nowhere to sit. Since then I'd done work for a leprechaun, and there for a while I thought my cousin had been turned into a bunny rabbit. I kept hoping for non-magical clients, but since that didn't look like it was going to happen anytime soon, Diz and I bought a couple of wee-folk sized chairs from Fistler's Fine Furnishings, my favorite used-furniture store. My cousin, who thankfully had not been turned into a bunny rabbit, worked at Fistler's, and he got us a good deal.

"Do you want anything to drink?" I asked. "I have some eggnog."

The eggnog was leftover from the Moretown Bay annual Holly Jolly Eggnog Festival. I wouldn't have braved the holiday crowds at the waterfront shopping district just to buy eggnog, but the masseuse across the street brought some back for Diz and I. I think she was hoping we'd reciprocate by booking a couple of her holiday stress-relief specials. The holiday massages came complete with brownies, which I was pretty sure were higher octane than the grocery store variety. Besides, the masseuse always offered us a two-for-one deal so I'd be sure to bring Diz with me. I didn't blame her. I'd take whatever chance I could get to see my partner in a towel, too. Diz bears more than a passing resemblance to The Rock, if The Rock had pointy ears and a cinnamon-colored mullet, that is.

Special brownies, a massage to die for, and a sexy, half-naked elf. I gave serious thought to booking massages for the both of us until I balanced our checkbook. So much for that bright idea. Maybe we could squeeze massages into the budget next year.

The eggnog the masseuse had given us was one of the few non-alcoholic varieties available at the festival. I don't normally offer my clients an honest-to-God drink, but it was Christmas Eve, and Merry looked pretty upset. Detectives in all the old pulps always had a bottle of Scotch tucked away in their desk drawer. Not that I was a detective in an old pulp and wasn't brandy what you were supposed to put in eggnog? Still...

"Do you want something a little more potent than plain eggnog?" I asked, and then I peered at her. "Are you even old enough for that?" She looked about four years old, but with magic folk, looks can be deceiving.

"Plain eggnog is fine," she said. "I'm only four hundred and seventy-six. I can't have those kinds of drinks for another twenty-four years." She said it like the legal drinking age for Santa's elves was common knowledge. It probably was at the North Pole.

Which was where Merry should be, especially on Christmas Eve.

I brought out two glasses of plain eggnog and a plate of almond cookies, a gift from the Asian store next to the office. Merry snatched one of the cookies off the plate and proceeded to devour it.

"Why are you involved with Baby New Year's mother

in the first place?" I asked as I plopped down one of my full-size chairs next to Merry. "Shouldn't you be helping Santa get ready for the big night?"

Merry grabbed another cookie, and I wondered if elves could get a sugar high.

"Foreign exchange program," she said, her mouth half full. "All of Santa's elves have to intern with another holiday before Hal offers us a permanent contract."

Hal was Santa's lawyer. He was also an elf, but since he had zero toy-making abilities, his parents had sent him to law school. I'd seen one of Hal's contracts. If I ever needed a lawyer, I was going to call him.

"It was either the Baby New Year program or the Anti-Valentine's Day division of Eros International." Merry scrunched up her button nose. "Can you see me in black lace and eyeliner?"

I couldn't. I also couldn't see Cupid's—excuse me— Eros's daughter Dyte working with Merry.

Dyte was in charge of all things Anti-Valentine's Day, thanks in no small part to me. Dyte wasn't so much a Goth as she was rebellious. The black clothes, black nail polish, and black hair weren't really fashion statements. She just hated the cheery, bow-and-arrow wielding, white-winged cherub that was her father's iconic image, and she really hated the fact that he licensed that image to all sorts of companies to help them promote Valentine's Day. I could commiserate. I didn't like Valentine's Day much myself. Perennial lack of romantic entanglements. Don't ask.

Well, Eros had made the mistake of putting his rebellious daughter in charge of one of the happy, cheery, corporate sell-out divisions of his international conglomerate. She'd promptly tried to run it into the ground before she ran away herself thanks to a broken heart caused by Daddy Dearest. After Diz and I found Dyte, I managed to negotiate a deal between her and Eros that gave the family an effective monopoly on all things Valentine's Day related, pro and con alike.

Merry would fit in Dyte's company about as well as a rosy-cheeked square peg would fit in a morose round hole. They'd end up making each other thoroughly miserable.

"Wise choice," I said. "But the last time I checked, foreign exchange students get paired up with a local so they don't get themselves in trouble, so why is Mama New Year's disappearance all your fault?"

Merry sighed again and brushed cookie crumbs off her red frock. "She wanted to go ice skating, but no one would let her. Too close to her due date, everyone was too nervous. They wouldn't even let her go outside by herself. You should have seen her, Dee. She was so sad. She told me she always went ice skating on Christmas Eve. Evan told me it was just the baby blues— Evan's my program host, he's ushered in all the Baby New Years this century, and he says the moms always get emotional right before the baby comes—but Santa always says nobody should be sad at Christmas. That's why we all work so hard at the North Pole, so everyone can have a happy Christmas. Exchange students are supposed to teach the host program something, too, so we all learn from each other."

I could see where this was going. "So you got her away from everyone and took her ice skating to make her happy," I said.

She squirmed in her chair. "Not exactly."

I raised an eyebrow. "What exactly did you do?"

"Well, they were right. It wouldn't have been safe for her to skate, so I took her to the aquarium so she could watch the penguins ice skate."

I blinked. The Moretown Bay Maritime Aquarium was a big-time tourist attraction down at the waterfront. The last time Santa's elves had been here, they'd avoided tourist areas like the plague. I didn't blame them. People stepped on me when I went out in crowds during the holidays, and I wasn't three feet nothing tall.

"The aquarium's swamped this time of year," I said. "I thought you didn't like crowds." That's why the elves had hired Diz and I to find Norman, after all.

"People give a really pregnant woman with a toddler a wide berth even at Christmas." She shrugged. "I can pass for a human child when I want to. I just have to pull the hat down to cover my ears."

True. Merry's ears were slightly pointed, but at the right angle and with her curly hair, those points were easy to miss. Plus, people saw what they expected to see, and mostly they expected to see people who looked like them.

Two things occurred to me then. The first was that I didn't know penguins ice-skated. The second, and more important thing as far as the investigation went, was that I'd assumed they'd gone to the aquarium down on the waterfront and Merry hadn't corrected me.

"Wait a minute," I said. "You took her to our aquarium, right? The Moretown Bay aquarium?"

Merry nodded.

"Baby New Year's mother lives here?" I asked.

"Until Baby New Year's born, then she can go back home to Michigan. That's where she's from."

"Then why is she... was she... here?"

Merry looked at me, clearly confused. "This is where the New Year's Institute is. You didn't know that?"

"Uh... no." I'd never heard of the New Year's Institute. Then again, before I met Eros, I'd never heard of Eros International either.

"We have to find her," Merry said. "She ditched me at the aquarium. She said she was just going to the bathroom—she has to do that a lot—but I never saw her come out, and when I went in to find her, she was gone." Her green eyes glistened with unshed tears. "Santa will be so disappointed in me. All I wanted to do was make her happy, but if we don't find her, this year might never end."

What? "Never end? Won't Baby New Year be born anyway?" Granted, I had no personal experience with pregnancy and babies, but I was sure that when the time came, that baby was coming out no matter where the mother happened to be.

"If he's not born at the Institute, he'll be just a regular baby, not Baby New Year," she said. "Last year's baby won't get to retire, which means he'll be cranky—well, crankier—because he can't be next year because he's this year, and everyone will have to do this whole year all over again."

The whole thing all over again. This had been an election year. For three months, we got more political calls than client calls at the office. Diz had been about ready to yank the phone out of the wall.

"Can you help me?" Merry said. "You're the only private detective I know. Can you find her?"

I'd been looking forward to a nice quiet evening with my cat and a peaceful Christmas morning curled up with a good book before I headed over to my mother's for Christmas dinner. In fact, I'd been about ready to call it a day when Merry had walked in my door. It was tempting to tell her no, but I didn't get in this business to tell people no, especially not repeat customers. Besides, I sure didn't want to live last year all over again. Except, you know, for that one time when my partner and I did go to the masseuse for one of her two-for-one massages.

Have I mentioned that my partner is gorgeous, and it's been a really, really long time since I've had a date?

I nodded at Merry. "Okay," I said. "We'll do our best."

"LET ME GET THIS RIGHT," Diz said. "You took a job on Christmas Eve."

The glower was on a slow simmer. I didn't know what plans my partner had for Christmas Eve, but he clearly wasn't happy that looking for a missing pregnant woman had just become one of them.

I smiled sweetly at him. "You want to live this last year all over again?"

"You could have asked me before you said yes."

"You would have said no."

Diz crossed his arms over his chest. "I can still say no."

"And leave me out there on my own? In the middle of a town full of last-minute shoppers?" I put one hand over my heart. "That hurts, Diz."

Okay, that was going overboard, even for me, but at least his glower hadn't deepened into a full-out glare. The last thing I wanted for Christmas was a truly angry partner. Diz doesn't have the most even temper in the world. Back when we were both detectives with the Moretown Bay police department, he used to play bad cop to my good cop. For him, it wasn't much of a stretch.

Although I do have to say that Diz has lightened up a lot since we opened the agency. Not that he's lost the glower, but I have caught him smiling a couple of times when he didn't know I was looking.

"Okay," he said with a sigh. "You got anything?"

Diz wasn't asking about my online search, even though I had five different browser windows open on my computer.

He was asking whether I'd had a vision about our missing mother-to-be.

I have a touch of precognition, and when I say "touch," I mean an annoyingly unreliable, uncontrollable ability to see little glimpses of the future. Sometimes.

My ability had apparently decided to take the holiday off. I'd tried concentrating on the cell phone picture Merry had snapped of Mama New Year at the aquarium to see if I could get a hint about where Baby New Year's mother would be or what she might be doing in the near future besides having a baby. As usual, all I'd gotten for my efforts was a headache.

"Nope," I said. "I've been trying to dig things up the old-fashioned way."

"Google," Diz said.

I grimaced. "Yup." Not that I'd come up with a whole lot that way either.

Mama New Year's real name was Betty Wallace. She was from Hollow Creek, a little town outside of Deerfield, Michigan, which, according to the Internet, was best known as the birthplace of Danny Thomas. Betty was twenty years old, blonde-haired and blue-eyed, and in the picture she was hugely pregnant.

While the Internet gave me thousands of hits on the name Betty Wallace, I got no returns at all when I tried narrowing my search to include either Michigan or Moretown Bay. Old-fashioned phone calls to the people I knew at all the local hospitals didn't net any results either, and no women matching Betty's description been picked up by the police or, thank goodness, the coroner's office.

Before she came to our office, Merry had already tried

179

to find Betty at the public skating rink the city set up for the winter at Broad Street Square. I figured Diz and I could swing by to check it out for ourselves. Just because Merry hadn't seen Betty didn't mean she wasn't there. Crowd three or four people around someone Merry's size and she wouldn't be able to see much of anything except winter coats and shopping bags.

On a hunch, I brought up Merry's picture of Betty on my computer and enlarged it. When Merry had snapped the picture, Betty had been staring at something off camera. There was something in her expression, a kind of wistful sadness, that I didn't think was due to watching penguins slide around on climate-controlled ice. I always thought penguins were kind of funny, myself.

Diz leaned over my shoulder to peer at the picture.

"See anything?" I asked.

"A very pregnant woman."

"No kidding. Anything else?"

He squinted. "Penguins on ice?"

Even I could see that. "I thought you told me elves had super-human eyesight."

"I said humans have sub-par eyesight."

"Same difference." I leaned closer to the screen. "What about that?" I asked.

Behind the clear Plexiglas that separated the penguins' enclosure from the gawking tourists watching them, a family drama was taking place. A smaller penguin had fallen on the ice. Two larger penguins stood over it. The camera had caught the larger penguins in mid-squabble, their mouths open and wings flapping.

A while back a cute little video of a penguin deliberately tripping another penguin had made the rounds on the Internet. I wondered if that was what had happened at the aquarium, only the trippee had another penguin defending him from the trippor.

Or maybe what Betty had seen was a mother penguin defending her baby.

Merry had told me that Betty could go back home to Michigan after Baby New Year was born. Did that mean Betty had to give away her baby in order for him to become Baby New Year? If that was the case, we might have just discovered a clue about what turned a clandestine visit to the aquarium into Escape of the Baby Mama. Of course, that didn't help me figure out where Betty was now, but knowing her motives gave me a good idea about where she might be headed.

"We better check the airlines, bus, and train terminals," I told Diz. "I think she might be headed home."

SOME THINGS WERE MUCH EASIER to do when we were cops. BOLOs, for instance. Put a name in the program, transmit a picture if you had it, and just like that, every employee at all the airline ticket counters, bus terminals, and train stations were (theoretically) on the lookout for your missing person. These days Diz and I had to use cell phones, text messages, and a well-cultivated list of contacts we'd developed from years on the job.

By the time we'd finished talking to all our contacts,

figured out who was working on Christmas Eve, and sent the right people a copy of Betty's picture, daylight was fading fast. The masseuse across the street had already turned off the Christmas lights in her windows and locked up for the night. No two-for-one Christmas Eve massages for us this year. And maybe not next year either, since we'd be doing this year all over again if Diz and I couldn't find Betty Wallace and convince her to return to the Institute.

That's the part about missing persons work most clients don't understand. Sure, finding someone who doesn't want to be found isn't always a piece of cake, but that's not the whole job. When the person who went missing was an adult, there wasn't much we could do to force them to go back to their old life if they didn't want to. Diz and I aren't thugs. If Betty didn't want to return to the Institute, Diz wouldn't throw her over his shoulder and carry her back. She might have backed out on whatever agreement she had with the Institute, but then it would be up to the Institute to hire someone like Hal to sue her. Of course, by the time that happened, Baby New Year would be plain old Baby Wallace, and the whole thing would be a moot point.

I pinched the bridge of my nose and tried to ignore the headache that was threatening to explode my brain. I'd put too much effort into this for the whole thing to be a moot point, and besides, I didn't want to let Merry down, not on Christmas Eve. I could tell she thought her career was pretty much over, but she'd gone back to the Institute to face the music. She was one brave little elf.

No matter how much my head hurt, I couldn't just sit around waiting for one of our contacts to... well, contact us. I needed to do something.

Diz must have had the same idea. Either that or he was getting tired of watching my cat try to rip Christmas paper off the present Diz had brought back for her. The paper must have been the kind that was spelled to stay intact until December 25th because my cat's claws hadn't even made a dent. *Don't Open Until!* gift wrap had hit the market a couple of years ago and become an instant hit with parents of impatient kids everywhere.

"Here," Diz said, handing me my coat. "Let's go ice skating and see if we can spot our runaway."

The only public ice skating rink in the city was at Broad Street Square. The Square, which was really a rectangle, took up two city blocks of prime real estate at the southern end of Moretown Bay's downtown shopping district. The Square was a mixture of grassy areas dotted with trees and park benches, brick walkways, and concrete. While the waterfront shops near the aquarium had a unique, eclectic, New Age feel, most of the stores that bordered the Square were definitely upscale, pricey, and carried the exact same clothes you could find in any large city. Needless to say, on my budget, I never shopped there.

The city maintained the Square as a public park, a bit of nature in the midst of high-rise urban sprawl, where people who either shopped themselves out or who worked in nearby office buildings could relax while they ate their fill of hot dogs, pretzels, popcorn, pulled-pork sandwiches, fish tacos, or chili in mini sourdough bread bowls, all sold from food carts and kiosks located throughout the Square.

During the summer, flower and fresh-fruit vendors set up shop alongside the food carts, and buskers entertained the crowds. During the winter, the city set up an oval ice-skating rink in the center of the square. The city's official twenty-foot tall Christmas tree was at one end of the rink, and an equally-tall display with live trees honoring Winter Solstice was at the other.

By the time we got to the Square, the sun had disappeared behind a fog bank blanketing the Bay. The Christmas tree was lit with red and green and blue and white and orange lights and topped with a golden five-point star. The trees in the Winter Solstice display were enchanted so they appeared dusted with snow, and tiny fairies flitted around the branches like fireflies. Christmas carols played over speakers hidden throughout the Square, and I could have sworn I smelled hot chocolate and fresh-from-the-oven gingerbread cookies.

If we weren't here looking for a missing woman, the whole thing would have made me as glowy warm inside as a Thomas Kinkaid painting.

Last-minute shoppers still dashed through the Square, hurrying to the next shop on their list or heading off to wherever they parked their cars, their arms weighed down with shopping bags. I didn't see any pregnant women among them or even anyone who even bore a passing resemblance to Betty. When I glanced at Diz to see if he'd caught a glimpse of her—Diz is pretty tall, which gives him a serious advantage when we're trying to spot someone in a crowd—he shook his head no.

We made our way over to the ice rink, weaving through the crowd like we were changing lanes on the freeway during rush hour. I made it through without getting elbowed or accidentally belted with someone's overflowing shopping bag or stuffed-to-the-gills back-pack. I chalked that up to Diz's intimidating presence. On my own, I'd have been black and blue before I'd made it halfway across the Square.

Quite a few people were still out on the ice even this late on Christmas Eve. An ice rink isn't the easiest thing to maintain in a city like Moretown Bay. Winters in the Pacific Northwest are moderate. Even in the dead of winter, we get more rain than snow, and the rink didn't have a cover. Besides a kickass refrigeration unit, I figured the city had to enlist some serious magic to keep the rink going from Thanksgiving through the end of February. I guess the skaters wanted to take advantage of the ice no matter the holiday.

I still didn't see Betty anywhere.

Diz left me alone by the side of the rink. I thought he was just going to look at the crowd from a different vantage point, but a minute later he came back holding ice skates.

Two pairs of ice skates.

"Here," he said, handing over one pair. "You need to have some fun."

I blinked at him. "Are you serious?"

He looked serious, but then again, he always looked serious. "It's Christmas Eve."

"And we have a case," I said. "Missing pregnant woman? About-to-be-fired Santa's elf? Any of that ring a bell?"

He lifted an eyebrow in a damn good impersonation of The Rock. "Skates," he said. "Those are yours." He held up his hand. "These are mine."

The other pair of skates certainly was Diz sized.

The blades on my skates were ridiculously thin. I couldn't even wear high heels without the threat of serious ankle injury. All those TV shows with lady cops in their high, high heels? Please. Real cops wore sensible shoes. How in the world was I supposed to stay upright on these skinny little things?

"How am I supposed to stay upright these things?" I said.

"Don't worry. If you fall, I'll catch you before you hit the ice."

Diz could move very fast when he wanted to. Back when we had to chase suspects, he'd be across the street and down the next block before my foot even left the curb. He always told me it was an elf thing.

Wait a minute. "Can't you just skate around on the ice anytime you want to? Isn't that an elf thing, too?"

He sighed. "I can walk on ice. If I want to glide over ice, I need skates just like everyone else." His glower was revving up. "Just put the damn things on."

Fine. I sat on a bench next to the rink and put the damn things on.

When I was done, Diz took my shoes and shoved them inside the deep pockets of his overcoat. He didn't take his own boots off. Instead, his boots seemed to merge with the skates.

Huh. I'd never realized before that my partner wore enchanted boots. Maybe that was why he never tracked water into the office no matter how hard it rained.

Or how he managed to scale the outside of buildings like he was walking up the side of a hill.

Elf thing, my ass.

Diz offered me his arm. I grabbed on like he was my own personal lifeboat.

"My mother's going to be annoyed with you when I end up with a broken leg for Christmas," I told him as I got unsteadily to my feet.

He snorted, a decidedly un-elfen sound.

He was right. As far as my mother was concerned, Diz could do no wrong. If I broke my leg, she'd be annoyed at me.

Somehow we made it out onto the ice. My ankles actually felt fairly stable thanks to the tight lace job on the boot part of the skates. My feet were another thing altogether. I still felt like my feet were going to go sailing out from under me at any moment.

I never had skates of any kind when I was a kid, and I'd only tried skateboarding once. A boy I'd liked let me try his skateboard, and because I wanted him to think I was cool so he'd like me back, I'd pretended to know what I was doing. I actually made it down my parents' driveway, missed the turn onto the sidewalk, and sailed out into the street. Luckily there'd been no traffic. I'd felt pretty good about myself until the skateboard hit a stone, came to an abrupt stop, and I went flying.

The bruises had been fairly impressive, and so, apparently, had been the emergency room bill since my mother insisted on getting my sprained ankle x-rayed just in case. The boy with the skateboard avoided me like the plague after that.

So when Diz told me he'd do all the work and all I had to do was hang on, I was more than willing to do an impersonation of a mannequin and let him haul me around the rink. I didn't care how ridiculous I looked. I just wanted to stay on my feet.

The third time around the rink, Diz looked down at me. He wasn't glowering, but he was frowning. "This is supposed to be fun," he said.

My legs were beginning to ache from the strain of trying to keep my balance. "I can have fun curled up with a good book. Eating Chinese food."

"We've done that."

True. Diz and I have spent a considerable amount of time together doing nothing more than reading, my cat perched happily on his shoulder, purring up a storm. We've also shared more meals together than I can count while we watched movies on the dinky old television my mother had picked up for me at a garage sale last summer. I enjoyed doing those things by myself, but doing them with Diz just made them more fun. I've mentioned that he's gorgeous, right? He also has the cutest pointy ears, which are on constant display thanks to his mullet. Not that I'd ever tell him his ears are cute.

"I thought you should try something I enjoy," he said.

Diz liked to ice skate? That was news to me.

Or was it something more than that?

This time as we skated around the rink, I quit looking at my feet and paid attention to Diz instead.

Elves are ridiculously graceful, even elves as solidly built at Diz. It's just part of their nature. Diz could outrun, out-muscle, and pretty much out-anything a suspect threw at him back when we were cops and he made it look easy. He'd been a crack shot, acing his qualifiers every year he'd been on the force. I'm pretty sure that if he ever had to use a bow and arrows or a set of fighting knives like the elves in those movies, he'd have been great at that, too, but it never occurred to me before that he enjoyed doing these things while he was doing them as much as he enjoyed the end result.

Me, I'm a goal-oriented person. Whatever process I had to go through to get results was just that—a process I had to go through. Even when I read a book or watched a movie, what I cared about was getting to the end to see how the whole thing turned out.

As I watched Diz, I realized he was enjoying himself. Sure, he wasn't grinning ear to ear, but the expression on his face was one of quiet contentment. Even with clumsy me hanging onto him for dear life, just using his natural grace and balance to skate around the rink was making him happy.

And he wanted to share that with me.

All of a sudden, I felt very small and humble.

"Thank you," I said. "This is a pretty cool Christmas gift. And here I didn't get you anything."

He made a sound that could have been a chuckle, but his only other response was to pick up the pace. I tried not to squeal as the fence on the edge of the rink slid by faster.

Now that I realized what Diz was up to, I had to admit that I didn't exactly hate being out on the ice. The little ball of tension in my belly wasn't much different than what I felt riding a Ferris wheel. My headache had faded, and I was entertaining the idea of moving at least one skate on my own just to see what it felt like. Diz did say he'd catch me if I fell.

I wished I had Diz's athletic abilities. If I was actually good at this kind of thing, I might learn to enjoy the doing-it portion more since I was pretty sure the end result of this particular process was going to be sore muscles in places I didn't even know I had muscles.

If only Diz could help me get a handle on my own precog ability. I'd probably enjoy it more if I had some control over the process. How can you enjoy something when you don't know when it's going to pounce on you? If it remains stubbornly off stage when you really need it to perform? If the precog visions were a natural part of me like Diz's athleticism and grace, how come I couldn't control them?

We zipped past the Christmas tree, the lights a blur of colors. My mother's tree would be a miniature version of that, complete with presents for me and the cousins. Usually my mother gave me things that were cute and frilly and totally not me, and that my cat either destroyed or slept on when I wasn't around. I didn't blame my mother. What she really wanted was a normal daughter who'd give her grandchildren. What she got was me.

And what did I want for Christmas? Besides spending quality time with Diz (which I was doing now) and having my cat actually sleep on my shoulders instead of his for a change (which was never going to happen)?

I wanted my damn ability to work when I wanted it to.

And just like that, it did.

Diz caught me before my head hit the ice just like he said he would, but I never knew it. The vision took me that fast and that completely.

What's a precog vision like? Well, most of the time I just get little hints of things. A smell that doesn't belong. A glimpse of something out of the corner of my eye that's gone as soon as I try to focus on it. Those kind of visions are almost like an overlay of the real world, and I can keep functioning right through them.

At other times, I get a silent movie, and the action on the screen is jerky and sepia toned. Or I get a series of disjointed images, like someone's flipping through a photo album too fast for me to concentrate on any one picture. Those visions blank out the real world for a moment or two. This explains why I usually let Diz do the driving.

The best visions I've ever had are full-blown movies, picture and sound in brilliant 3-D, so real that I forget I belong anywhere else. The first time that happened it scared the crap out of me. I'm used to them now, not that I've had all that many visions like that.

The vision that hit me at the rink wasn't like any vision I'd had before.

This one made me feel like I was piggybacking on someone's dream, and I was the Ghost of Christmas Present.

The vision started out in a maternity ward nursery, only instead of rows of basinets filled with crying, cooing, or sleeping babies all cocooned in pink or blue blankets, this nursery contained only one basinet. It sat empty in the center of the room, a blue blanket draped over its clear plastic sides. The walls of the nursery were decorated with posters of the babies who'd occupied the basinet in years past. Most of the artwork in the posters looked like something Norman Rockwell might have painted, but the banner beneath each of the babies was emblazoned with a year that dated back to before the Second World War.

The nursery wasn't quite empty. An ancient man stood next to the empty basinet. He wasn't dressed in hospital scrubs. Instead he wore a rumpled suit that looked two sizes too big. His red-and-blue striped tie hung loose around his neck, and he stood hunched over, his weight supported by a crooked cane, a look of profound sorrow on his lined face.

The old man seemed to be muttering to himself, but before I could make out the words, the room winked out and I was floating above the ground, my toes skimming over damp grass.

It was nighttime, and cold. My breath puffed out in front of me but I didn't feel cold, which I should have considering I was dressed in Merry's sleeveless red frock. I still had ice stakes on my feet, and I had a sneaking suspicion I had Merry's hat on my head because a white pompom bobbed along at the top of my field of vision.

I was headed toward a glowing shape on the horizon. Christmas carols drifted toward me on the night air, voices accompanied by a single piano and guitar. The music didn't have that piped-in, pre-recorded quality like in the Square. One of the sopranos went off-key on the high notes, and a tenor couldn't quite keep to the tempo set by the musicians. What the singers lacked in expertise, they certainly made up for in enthusiasm. When people talked about a joyful noise, this was it.

I wasn't alone in the dark. Instead, I was gliding along next to a hugely pregnant woman. She could have been Betty, but instead of the navy blue coat Betty had been wearing in Merry's picture, this woman wore a long robe complete with a hood that obscured her face. I tried to peer around the hood, but dream me refused to cooperate.

Time has no meaning in dreams, and neither does continuity. One moment I was floating without hurry toward the distant glow, trying to peer at my companion, and the next I stood on the other side of her in front of a holiday scene that was familiar even to someone like me who never set foot inside a church except under protest. The glow had resolved itself to floodlights reflecting off the inside of a high-peaked roof. The ground beneath the roof was covered with straw and surrounded on three sides by temporary plywood walls to create an open-air stage for actors who stood as still as mannequins in their robes and fake beards. One woman draped in a powder-blue robe knelt on the ground next to an empty cradle. I knew a baby would appear in that cradle at midnight.

No donkeys or sheep or other barnyard animals were in attendance, but a large Golden Retriever kept watch over the scene. A young boy holding a shepherd's staff stood next to the dog, his attention on that empty cradle.

A low rope fence separated the scene from passersby. My companion and I stood near the fence just shy of the warm circle of light that illuminated the scene. She sighed deeply and rubbed a protective hand over her belly. Snow began to fall, large fluffy flakes that coated the ground and landed wetly on my nose.

The dog lifted its head to the sky, a grin on its doggy face. Then it turned to look directly at me.

"Time to wake up," it said, still grinning.

"Time to wake up," Diz said.

194

I blinked and tried to focus. Diz had an arm around my shoulders and was peering down at me.

"You were snoring," he said.

We were still at the ice rink. I was sitting—or more precisely, I was sprawled—on the bench where I'd first put on my skates, only now I was leaning against Diz who was sitting next to me. People passing by were pointedly ignoring us, which made me guess that anyone who'd expressed concern about the fact that I'd basically passed out on the rink had earned a high-octane glare from my partner.

"I wasn't asleep," I said, even though the last word came out around a huge yawn.

A frown built between Diz's eyebrows. "Vision?"

"Yeah."

"Useful?"

I sat up and reached for the laces on my skates. "Well, I think I know where our missing baby mama's going to be," I said as I took the skates off. Where we were going, we wouldn't need the skates. "And I'm pretty sure we're going to have a white Christmas."

Diz narrowed his eyes at me. I could count the number of times Moretown Bay had had a white Christmas on no fingers.

"Are you sure you weren't just dreaming?" he asked.

Well, I'd either had a vision or I'd developed a sudden case of narcolepsy. Since narcolepsy wasn't at all helpful to the case, I was going with vision.

"I'm sure," I said.

Moretown Bay has its fair share of churches, but only

one sponsors a living nativity scene. Diz blinked at me when I told him what I'd seen in my vision, then he hailed a cab. The nativity scene was in the suburbs. I wondered how Betty'd even heard about it.

There are still people in the world who think that magic and religion don't mix. One night when Diz and I had been on a long, boring stake-out and the conversation had turned to serious topics, Diz told me that religious zealotry was one of the reasons magic folk had kept mostly to themselves throughout the centuries. Sure, ancient gods like Eros didn't care one way or the other whether humans knew they existed, but other magic folk—the elves and fairies and goblins and dwarves, and hundreds of others—lived unnoticed in the mortal world, and they liked it that way. Apparently things like The Crusades and The Inquisition had scared the crap out of them. I didn't blame them.

Only when industrialization and expansionism had threatened their way of life did magic folk feel compelled to reveal their existence to the human world. The world's religions had scrambled to redefine themselves and reinterpret their governing texts to encompass the fact that magic really existed, although some continued to insist that there were two sides to that particular fact, and those of us who acknowledged that elves like Diz were real and even mortals like me could possess magical abilities were delusional.

These days most religions had come to terms with the existence of magic folk, at least enough to coexist in peace around the holidays. That's why the city had both a Christmas tree and a Winter Solstice display in Broad Street Square. Leprechauns owned manufacturing companies that produced shoes for the entire country, and the God of Love's daughter operated one of her father's international conglomerates for the sole purpose of flooding the market with anti-Valentine's Day products. Churches still celebrated midnight mass on Christmas Eve, and actors in a live nativity scene still awaited the arrival of a certain baby at midnight.

By the time the cab dropped us off at the suburban park where the nativity scene was set up, the first fat flakes of snow had begun to fall from the night sky.

"See?" I said to Diz.

He glowered at me. "Don't get cocky. Even if she's here, that doesn't mean we can convince her to go back."

Tell me something I didn't know. Visions could only get us so far.

I put up the hood on my coat, and we found a spot off to the side where we could blend in with everyone else who stopped to see the nativity scene.

The nativity looked pretty much like it had in my vision, only without the Golden Retriever. The woman playing Mary was sitting rather than kneeling next to the empty cradle—much easier on the knees—and instead of one lone shepherd, a group huddled together not watching over their flocks by night. All of them held hooked staffs that looked like giant candy canes spray painted gold.

On the far side of the group of actors clustered around the cradle, six carol singers stood beneath a portable canopy bravely belting out Christmas standards accompanied only by a guitar player who wore fingerless gloves. The soprano was still off-key on the high notes— I saw Diz wince every time she tried—and the tenor still couldn't keep a beat.

Most of the people who stopped to look at the nativity scene were clearly on their way somewhere else. Some had the same kind of shopping bags I'd seen in the Square, only these were from discount stores and mall shops. Others were dressed for church. Thanks to my mother, I knew that the interfaith church that sponsored the living nativity held its services in what used to be a buffet-type restaurant around the corner. I'd never been inside, but Mother told me they'd gutted the place, put in new carpet, and made it "quite lovely." She'd apparently gone to one of their services with her neighbor, the same one who read Tarot cards for all the ladies in the neighborhood. When this particular church said they were all inclusive, I guessed they really meant it.

Diz noticed Betty first, but that wasn't surprising. He had far better night vision than I did. Instead of saying anything, he just nudged me in the ribs, and all I had to do was follow his gaze.

Betty was still wearing the same coat she'd had on in Merry's picture. She had a knitted scarf pulled up over her head, and she looked weary beyond belief. I wondered where she'd been all afternoon and if she'd had a chance to take a nap. When my perfect cousin Stacy had been about ready to deliver the first of her two perfect children, she must have slept eighteen hours a day—when she wasn't baking homemade bread and knitting baby booties, that is. My mother said it was part of the nesting instinct. I took her word for it. At the rate I was going, I doubted I'd ever experience childbirth first hand.

Our missing mother-to-be stopped in front of the nativity scene. She rubbed a protective hand over her belly. She didn't seem to notice the snow settling on the shoulders of her coat or on the fringe of blonde hair that had escaped from beneath the scarf. She also didn't seem to notice the other people who'd gathered to watch the nativity. Her gaze was fixed on that empty cradle.

I sighed. This was the hard part, and it was something I had to do by myself. I didn't want Diz to spook her. It was time for the good cop to earn her living. Not that Merry was paying us. If this went well, I figured I could invoice Hal later, or get a grateful Institute to foot the bill.

If there was a later, that is, and not a year of do-overs.

I strolled along the outside edge of the nativity scene until I reached Betty. I didn't look directly at her, but I didn't think she would have noticed even if I had. Her gaze was still riveted on the nativity scene, but I'd been wrong about what she was looking at. The empty cradle wasn't the center of her attention.

Betty's gaze was riveted on the woman playing Mary.

I could have tried to make small talk with her, but that didn't feel right. I wasn't religious in the least, but it still felt wrong to try to mislead her on Christmas Eve, especially here.

"I'm a friend of Merry's," I said.

Betty blinked. "Mary?" She glanced at me and then back toward the actors. "You mean..."

"Oh. No." I held up my hand, Santa-elf high. "Merry. Button nose. Brown curls. Four hundred, seventy-six years old. That Merry."

"Oh," Betty said. She went back to staring at the nativity. "Is she in trouble?"

I lifted an eyebrow. "Yeah, I kinda think she is."

"Oh," she said again, and she heaved a sigh. "I didn't mean to get her in trouble. I just needed some time by myself to think." She was still rubbing her belly with one hand. "Are you going to take me back?"

"Only if you want to go," I said. "My partner and I were hired to find you, not kidnap you." I nodded toward Diz. "We'll make sure you get back safely if you decide that's what you want. If you don't?" I shrugged. "We'll tell Merry you're all right, and that will be that."

I could see her think about that. Her eyes had widened when she'd looked at Diz, but the fact that he'd stayed where he was seemed to reassure her.

She went back to watching nativity Mary. Those thick, fluffy flakes of snow were still falling. The ground was turning white, my nose was cold, and I couldn't feel my toes. I was going to need a long, hot shower and something hot to drink when I got back to my little apartment over the office.

"Do you think she knew?" Betty asked.

I didn't have to ask who she meant. She was still staring at Mary.

"Knew what?" I asked.

"When her baby was born, do you think she knew what kind of a life he was in for?" Her hand was splayed protectively over her belly.

I might not know anything about the Bible beyond knowing that there have been a bunch of different versions of it, but it wasn't hard to figure out what Betty was talking about. Mary's baby had indeed had a rough life.

"Nobody knows what kind of life their baby's in for," I said. After all, my mother was still waiting for her first grandchild, and since all her proverbial eggs were in my basket, it looked like she'd be waiting for a very long time.

"I do," Betty said, her voice very small and sad. "I know. I always knew, or at least I thought I did until This Year came back."

This Year. Did she meant the rumpled old man I'd seen in my vision? Didn't they usually go by the names of their year?

"He's so used up," she said. "Is my baby going to hate me for doing that to him?"

Things were starting to make sense. Betty had been fine knowing her baby would be the next Baby New Year right up until she got a first-hand look at the old man who'd been last year's baby.

"I didn't think it would matter this much, you know? I never even wanted kids. I wasn't supposed to get... I mean, we used stuff and everything just like we were supposed to. It should have worked, and when it didn't and he left me..." She sighed. "This whole thing was just supposed to be an adventure. The Institute really wanted him and I didn't, and they agreed to pay to bring me out here and have the baby here even though I was older than most of the moms. I always wanted to live by the ocean. It all seemed perfect."

She was still so very young. I had to remind myself that I was only seven years older than she was.

And most of the moms had been younger than she was? "You're not that old," I said.

"For them, I am."

"Why?" A decision like that would be hard for a woman any age to make, much less a girl who hadn't really lived much of a life yet.

She turned toward me and seemed to study my face. "You really don't know."

"I don't know much of anything about this. Until Merry came to see me today, I didn't even know there was a real Baby New Year. I thought it was just an advertising gimmick. Like the Energizer Bunny." Which Diz had assured me was not real. Unlike the Easter Bunny, who was.

She shifted her weight, and I could tell she was trying to ease the strain on her back. I thought about offering to take her someplace where she could sit down, but I didn't think she was ready to leave the nativity. Not just yet.

"What did Merry tell you?" she asked.

"That if your baby's not born at the Institute, he'll be a regular baby and last year will happen all over again."

"That's right," she said. "I don't go through with it, and congratulations to me, I've screwed up another year —only for everybody this time. But if I do?" Her hand was back to rubbing her belly. "If I do, next Christmas Eve my baby will look just like This Year. He'll only be a year old, but he might as well be my grandfather."

I realized Betty was like most kids her age. They all thought they were the center of the universe, and maybe the Institute counted on that. Betty had made a decision based on what was best for her, and it wasn't until now, with a week left to go, that she'd thought about what that deal would mean for her son.

"You're afraid he'll hate you because he'll live an entire lifetime over the space of one year," I said.

She laughed, a bitter sound. "That's only part of it. After a new baby takes his place and he gets to retire, his life goes backward. He gets younger. When I'm forty, he'll be my father's age. By the time I hit sixty, he'll look like my college-age son."

I blinked as the implications of that hit me. "When you're eighty, he'll be a toddler," I said.

She nodded.

She was still thinking in terms of herself, but at least not just about herself. She'd discovered she wanted a relationship with her unborn son, a child she'd thought was just an inconvenience to be dealt with and then forgotten. Maternal instinct might have kicked in late, but at least it had kicked in.

I thought about the penguins at the aquarium. When Betty's son finally got young enough to need protecting from neighborhood bullies, or when he might have broken his ankle trying to skateboard down a driveway, she'd be too old to take him to the emergency room and hold him while he cried, more embarrassed than hurt.

"He's never going to be a little boy with you," I said.

Her eyes glistened with unshed tears. "No, he's not. I never thought that mattered, and it didn't before, but it's Christmas Eve, and now I know, I really know, that I'm never going to see him run down the stairs first thing on Christmas morning, so excited to see what Santa left for him. I'm going to miss all that."

But she didn't have to miss all that. She still had a chance to be a mother to a normal son. I knew I was supposed to talk her into going back to The Institute. That was the result I was supposed to get for my client, and I was all about results, wasn't I? But I couldn't do it. Not this time.

"I'm sorry," I said. "I shouldn't have bothered you. You have enough on your mind. I'll just tell Merry that you're fine, and you can—"

"Lovely night, isn't it?"

I hadn't heard the man come up behind us, and from the startled look on Betty's face, she hadn't either. He was in his mid-forties and a little taller than I was. His cheeks were ruddy with the cold, and he wore a familiar-looking leather jacket and a battered brown leather fedora.

"I always like coming to the nativity scene when I'm in town visiting my mother for the holidays," he said. "In my day, someone always volunteered a real baby to play the part, but these days they use one of those disturbingly lifelike dolls. Probably better for everyone involved, but I do miss the arrival of a real baby."

His blue eyes were a little faded, but laugh lines crinkled at the corners, and I swore I saw a hint of wicked good humor play at the corners of his mouth. I wondered how much of our conversation he'd heard.

"A real baby," Betty said. "Yeah. A real baby would be nice."

"Don't worry," the man said. "You're going to be a wonderful mother, if an unconventional one."

Betty blinked at him. "What?"

The man had been listening to us.

I shot a look at Diz. I wanted him to be ready in case there was trouble. He was watching us intently, a frown on his face, but all of a sudden the frown smoothed out. He nodded at the nativity scene.

I turned around in time to see a middle-aged woman handing a lifelike baby doll to one of the shepherds in the nativity, who in turn handed the doll to Mary. The crowd of onlookers applauded, and the carol singers launched into a mostly on-key rendition of "Joy to the World!"

"Wonderful job, as usual," the man said as the middle-aged woman walked over to us. "I was just talking to..."

He looked at Betty, clearly waiting for her to give him her name. She did.

"Talking to Betty here," he said to the woman. "I think she's a little worried about the choice she made for her son."

Wait a minute. "I don't mean to be rude, but—"

"You're not, dear," the woman said. "He does that a lot, but I think he still believes it's his job."

"To eavesdrop?"

"To take care of everyone," she said. "It's a hard habit to break." She turned her attention to the man. "It's about time to go in for the service." She reached up to smooth the collar of his jacket. "Are you warm enough in that? I keep telling you I'll get you a coat that has a decent lining. You're going to catch your death of cold out here."

The man gave me a *what can you do?* shrug that was as familiar as his coat and hat, and a light bulb went off in my brain.

I'd thought the middle-aged woman was his wife. She wasn't.

She was his mother.

"What year?" I asked him.

He grinned, dipped his head a bit, and touched the brim of his hat. "Nineteen eighty-one."

I knew now why the jacket and fedora looked so familiar. "What happened to the whip?" I asked him.

He beamed at me. "She never let me get one. Said it would give people the wrong impression."

Nineteen Eighty-One offered his mother an arm, and she tucked her hand in the crook of his elbow. Together they joined a group of people heading toward the church.

"He was a Baby New Year," Betty said, watching them go.

"Yup." Nineteen eighty-one had been the year one of

206

my mother's favorite movies had come out. The movie was before my time, but she still had a crush on Harrison Ford to this day.

"And he still talks to his mother," Betty said.

"Sure looks like it."

I could have pressed the point, but Betty needed time to come to her own conclusions.

She watched the nativity scene until the carol singers finished the last song of the night, the guitar player packed his guitar away, and the nativity actors dropped out of character to hug each other and wish each other a Merry Christmas. By that time, my nose had gone numb and I was shivering inside my coat, but at least it had finally stopped snowing. By morning, all trace of the snow would probably be gone. Snow didn't last long in Moretown Bay.

"Okay," Betty finally said, turning toward me. "Can you take me back?" She took a deep breath. "There's a cute little elf I really need to apologize to."

DIZ OFFERED to take Betty back to The Institute and stay with her until she was settled. I expected her to balk, but apparently she decided that having a grumpy elf for backup would discourage anyone from getting too angry with her. I almost went along just for the amusement factor, but it was nearly two in the morning. I was wet and cold and seriously tired, and I still wanted a hot shower.

Diz had the cab swing by the office to drop me off, and we all said Merry Christmas to each other. Betty even gave me an awkward, baby-in-the-way hug.

"I have to ask," I said to her before she got back in the cab. "How did you know about the nativity scene?"

She shrugged. "I don't remember exactly, but I had a dream about the nativity my mom always sets up at Christmas, and I just really wanted a nativity for Christmas. I saw a flyer at the aquarium for this one."

"A dream," Diz said, looking at me.

I arched my eyebrow the way he always did. "Vision."

Diz almost smiled, but he caught himself. "Talk to you tomorrow," he said.

When I unlocked the door to my apartment, the first thing I saw was shredded bits of wrapping paper. Of course. The paper on my cat's present was only spelled to last until Christmas, and technically it was Christmas Day. I followed a trail of catnip and toy mouse guts to find my blissed-out cat in the middle of my bed. She even meowed at me.

"Merry Christmas yourself," I said.

I stayed in the shower longer than was strictly necessary, but the hot water felt marvelous sluicing over my sore muscles. My legs were still stiff from ice skating, if what I'd been doing could be called "skating," and I had a pretty good knot in between my shoulder blades.

One thing I didn't have, though, was a headache.

In fact, I hadn't had a headache since Diz and I were gliding around on the ice and I'd started to consider there might be more to life than focusing on results.

There was a lesson somewhere in all that, but I was too tired to think about the benefits of going all Zen on my goal-oriented self. I didn't even fix myself hot chocolate before I tumbled into bed next to my snoring cat.

Christmas morning started off with a phone call from my mother reminding me to make sure I brought eggnog for dinner. Luckily I still had some leftover festival eggnog because I'd completely forgotten to buy any to take to my mother's.

I slipped on my comfy plaid bathrobe, made myself long overdue hot chocolate, and padded downstairs to the office with one of the books I was currently reading. We had a live Christmas tree in the front office again this year, and my Christmas morning tradition was to curl up in a comfy spot and read. In the office, my comfy spot was the little loveseat next to the tree.

I'd read about three pages when something scratched at the office door. I looked up from my book and saw the Golden Retriever from my vision staring at me through the glass door, a grin on his doggie face.

I nearly dropped the book.

When I didn't make a move toward the door, the dog tilted his head and scratched at the door again with one paw.

I got up, unlocked the door, and opened it a crack. "What are you doing here?" I asked.

I half expected him to talk to me like he did in my vision. Instead he chuffed at me, a sound that wasn't quite a bark, and he wagged his tail. When I didn't open the door any further, he shoved his nose against the open crack and pawed at the door again.

"I have a cat," I said. "She pretty much thinks she owns the place."

The dog looked up at me with big brown eyes and chuffed again.

My visions aren't always one hundred percent accurate, and that one had been all disjointed like most dreams were. For some reason, the vision had smooshed the dog together with the nativity scene instead of putting the dog in my office, where he clearly thought he belonged.

And maybe he did. What did I know? Until yesterday, I hadn't even known Baby New Year was a real baby.

Oh, what the hell.

I opened the door a little wider and the dog came in. His paws were wet, but he actually seemed to wipe them, in doggy fashion, on the mat we had right inside the front door. Someone must have trained him to do that, right?

I relocked the door and went back over to the loveseat while the dog sniffed around the front office. He sneezed once at the spot in the doorway between the front and back office where Diz usually leaned whenever he wanted to talk to me while I was at my desk, then he found a spot on the floor near the tree that must have satisfied his sensibilities. He turned in a tight circle three times before he laid down, head on his front paws, facing me.

"My cat's not going to be happy about this," I said.

He wagged the very tip of his tail, the doggy grin still on his face. I was beginning to think it was his natural expression. It made him look very content, all curled up in my office.

"You know I'm a cat person," I said.

He wagged his tail harder.

Oh, boy. It seemed I'd just been adopted by a dog.

A dog who'd talked to me in my vision.

This was going to be fun.

Newsletter Sign Up

Be the first to know!

If you love Annie's writing, her newsletter is a great way to keep up with new releases, special promotions, and bundles where her work is featured, not to mention the occasional giveaway that's only available to her newsletter subscribers. You'll even receive a free copy of the first Abby Maxon mystery novel, *Pretty Little Horses,* when you sign up!

What are you waiting for?

Sign up at https://anniereed.wordpress.com/newsletter/ today!

ALSO BY ANNIE REED

Eight from the Silver State

The Patient Z Files

The Forever Soldier and Other Future Tales

It's a Crime

WRITING AS KRIS SPARKS

Shadow Life

WRITING AS LIZ McKNIGHT

Wedding Belle Blues

ABOUT THE AUTHOR

ANNIE REED has been called "one of the best writers of her generation" and for good reason. She writes in multiple genres, including urban and contemporary fantasy; a variety of mystery subgenres, from hardboiled to cozy, including her popular Diz & Dee cozy paranormal mysteries; science fiction; contemporary romance; and thrillers. Sometimes she even writes a story that doesn't fall into any one specific category.

She's won awards as diverse as her writing. A multiple Derringer finalist, she's been honored with appearances in five year's best mystery and crime volumes, including an amazing three years in a row in the prestigious *BEST MYSTERY STORIES OF THE YEAR* (2022, 2023, and 2024) edited by Otto Penzler. She received a Silver Honorable Mention from Writers of the Future, a Literary Fellowship award, and one of her holiday romances was chosen to appear in study materials in Japan for students preparing for college entrance exams.

Annie's a founding member and frequent contributor to the innovative *UNCOLLECTED ANTHOLOGY*. Her stories appear regularly in *PULPHOUSE FICTION MAGAZINE,*

MYSTERY, CRIME & MAYHEM, and *THRILL RIDE – THE MAGAZINE*. Her recent novels include the *GRAY LADY RISING* series co-written with *USA Today* bestselling author Robert Jeschonek, the Abby Maxon mysteries, and *ROAD OF NO RETURN*. She's even written official *Star Trek* fiction and admits that she's an unabashed MCU fangirl.

She currently writes and edits fulltime. You can read all about her work on her website anniereed.wordpress.com. She also hangs out on Facebook as annie.reed.142.